"I____ ____ thanks."

"C___ ____
u____
r____
yourself, Ariel, ___ ____

"I'll carry you into the shower with me and make sure you don't fall."

Ariel stared at him, torn between annoyance and a perverse thrill of physical awareness. His masculinity seemed overwhelming in the confines of the bathroom, and she couldn't help thinking about what it would feel like to press up against his body when it was wet and slick with soap.

"Er…Mac. I can manage on my own, thanks. You can use the shower when I'm through. Close the bathroom door on your way out."

"We have already agreed that you can't manage on your own," he said, sounding puzzled and annoyed. "You might slip on a wet tile and fall. In view of your injured ankle, I must hold you while you wash, that is obvious."

Ariel blushed. "Mac, listen to me. Let's go through this one more time. In my world, men don't help women to take a shower when the two of them have just met. It's not the way things work in the nineties, okay?"

He shook his head. "The ways of your world are most foolish."

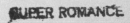

Harlequin Temptation is thrilled to introduce readers to **Jasmine Cresswell,** bestselling author of more than forty novels. Her efforts have earned her numerous awards, including the RWA's Golden Rose Award and the Author's League Award for best original paperback novel. Jasmine's books are favorites with readers all over the world, and we're happy that we can include *Midnight Fantasy* in their number.

Books by Jasmine Cresswell

HARLEQUIN INTRIGUE
194—NOWHERE TO HIDE
245—KEEPING SECRETS
297—EDGE OF ETERNITY

MIRA BOOKS
CHASE THE PAST
DESIRES & DECEPTIONS

Don't miss any of our special offers. Write to us at the following address for information on our newest releases.

Harlequin Reader Service
U.S.: 3010 Walden Ave., P.O. Box 1325, Buffalo, NY 14269
Canadian: P.O. Box 609, Fort Erie, Ont. L2A 5X3

Jasmine Cresswell
MIDNIGHT FANTASY

Harlequin Books

TORONTO • NEW YORK • LONDON
AMSTERDAM • PARIS • SYDNEY • HAMBURG
STOCKHOLM • ATHENS • TOKYO • MILAN
MADRID • WARSAW • BUDAPEST • AUCKLAND

ISBN 0-373-25674-4

MIDNIGHT FANTASY

1

ARIEL SQUEEZED between Elizabeth I of England and Lieutenant Commander Data, and sidestepped in time to avoid falling over Catwoman's whip. She circled two waiters, evaded a vampire who seemed determined to talk to her and finally made it over to the screened patio where Miranda was holding court for a crowd of admirers.

The Empress Josephine, Ariel thought with rueful affection. Trust her sister to come up with the perfect costume to show off her stunning beauty and stand out from the crowd by sheer simplicity.

Miranda glanced up and finally noticed her sister's arrival. She jumped from her chair in a flutter of semitransparent white silk. "Ariel, darling, you made it! I've been waiting for you all night!"

Every male eye within a ten-yard radius watched as Miranda waved to her sister with childlike enthusiasm. Her lustrous dark hair was piled high on her head, and heavy gold earrings—probably authentic late-eighteenth century—dangled to her naked shoulders, emphasizing the perfection of her magnolia skin and the tempting swell of her cosmetically uplifted breasts. Her nipples could be seen through the thin fabric of her costume, but the overall effect of her outfit was so restrained that a naive observer might wonder if this visibility was a mistake. Ariel, of course, knew better. Her sister had doubtless spent three or four hours in front of a mirror, changing the light from dim to bright, in order to ensure that the degree of transparency was exactly right.

Ariel had long ago given up trying to fathom where Miranda had acquired her amazing instincts for the precise boundaries of good taste. God knows, not from their parents. Tonight, despite the thrusting nipples and the naked shoulders, Miranda not only looked like every man's fantasy of chaste womanhood, she had somehow managed to make the rest of the women in the room appear overdressed and vulgar.

Except for me, Ariel reflected with a wry glance down at her plain black sheath. I just look dowdy.

Responding to her sister's wave, Ariel wound her way around Elvis and Jay Leno, taking care to nod politely in case either of them was the real thing. At Miranda's parties, you could never be sure. She returned her sister's hug with enthusiasm. She hated parties, especially Halloween costume parties, but she loved her sister.

"Hi, Miranda. You look wonderful. I'm green with envy over those earrings."

"Do you like them?" Miranda smiled, clearly thrilled with the compliment, even though Ariel could hardly be considered a fashion guru. "I found them in this terrific new antique shop by the beach. Do you want them? Here—"

"No, thank you. They look much better on you," Ariel cut in ruthlessly, knowing from experience that she couldn't hesitate or she'd be leaving the party wearing a thousand dollars' worth of earrings. Once started on the subject of shopping, and a terrific new boutique, Miranda was almost unstoppable, and her generosity could be overwhelming.

"What are you supposed to be?" Miranda asked, scowling at her sister's uninspired black dress.

"A witch," Ariel said.

Miranda rolled her eyes. "How splendidly original, darling. Where's your hat?"

"Here." Ariel held up a traditional pointed hat, which she'd found yesterday in the prop room of the PBS station where she worked. It was surprisingly well made, with an attached veil of thick black net, liberally decorated with silver stars and crescent moons.

"Why aren't you wearing it?" Miranda asked.

Because she was too damn self-conscious. "It was too tall to wear in the car," Ariel said.

"But you're not in the car now. Let me put it on you." Miranda adjusted the hat on her sister's head, unwinding the veil and giving it a couple of expert shakes so that the silver stars and moons settled around Ariel's black sheath in a faintly mysterious swirl.

Miranda stepped back, admiring her efforts. "There, that's much better. You look like the most frightening sort of witch—a real temptress."

"Thank you, I guess." Ariel was not comfortable with her sister's scrutiny. Any minute now, Miranda would summon a waiter and instruct him to find a broomstick, or a magic wand, or some gadget that spurted laser lights at the flash of a button. Ariel felt silly enough already, just wearing the hat. "Where's Ralph?" she asked. "I don't see him around."

Miranda's gaze flicked vaguely toward the marble staircase. "Somewhere upstairs," she said. "You know Ralph. When I give a party, he takes his cronies into a corner and they spend the evening plotting how to conquer the world widget market, or calculating the effect of interest rates on the ten-year Eurobond market."

Miranda's husband was forty-nine years old and a multimillionaire. On a scale of one to ten, his looks rated about a three, if you happened to be feeling generous. His social skills rated about a minus seven. He just didn't seem to be Miranda's type. One of the many subjects Ariel never discussed with her sister was why Miranda had chosen to marry him.

"I'll go and find him," Ariel said. She liked her brother-in-law's dry sense of humor and always enjoyed time spent in his company, even though he wasn't a man who encouraged intimacy. "I'll catch you later, Miranda, when you're not so busy."

"Don't go," Miranda said, giving an absentminded kiss to the Marquis de Sade, who strolled by escorting a young woman wearing jeweled handcuffs and three strategically placed leather patches. "I want you to meet a friend of mine. I invited him especially so the two of you could get acquainted."

Ariel barely conquered a groan. Damn, she thought. Here we go again. Another one of Miranda's walking wounded.

Her spirits perked up a bit when Miranda bypassed the Marquis de Sade and tugged on the sleeve of a tall, handsome man standing a couple of feet away from her. He was wearing a regular black-tie outfit, as opposed to fancy dress, and politely pretending not to eavesdrop. Ariel had the immediate impression that he felt as out of place as she did in this gathering of Hollywood industry insiders.

Miranda propelled him toward Ariel, her smile a tad overbright. "Jeff, this is my sister, Ariel. I'm sure you'll both have a lot in common. She produces documentaries for PBS, the real heavy-duty stuff." Miranda smiled with maternal pride. "She's an absolute genius, you know. Phi Beta Kappa, class valedictorian, graduate degree in communications, the works. We're all dreadfully intimidated by her."

Ariel winced, knowing all too well how most men reacted to hearing her intellectual pedigree, but Miranda grabbed her hand before she could murmur an excuse and run away.

"Jeff is the Washington correspondent for the *Los Angeles Post*," she said. "I know you admire his work, Ariel. He won a Pulitzer Prize for his coverage of President Clinton last year."

"Jeff Wolfman?" Ariel said, her interest caught. "It's certainly a pleasure to meet you, Jeff. I've admired your work for a long time."

Jeff gave a disarmingly modest grin. "Then it's mutual, Ariel. I've been looking forward to this all evening."

"He got divorced last year, and he's just your type," Miranda muttered in Ariel's ear. "An intellectual, honey. His brain's three times the size of his balls."

"Did you check that out personally?" Ariel murmured sweetly before turning with a resigned sigh to listen to whatever Jeff might have to say for himself.

He was smart enough to talk about her work before his, a definite point in his favor. "I saw your series on health-care reform last year," he said. "It was great stuff. That segment on the emergency room in an inner-city children's hospital was gut-wrenching. Great reporting."

"Thanks." Ariel smiled. "A compliment from you is definitely worth having."

"I knew you two would hit it off," Miranda said, smiling at them with the slightly anxious look of a mother duck waiting to see if her ducklings will manage to swim. Ariel, a veteran at handling her sister's matchmaking efforts, decided it was time to move out of Miranda's visual range.

"Would you be interested in taking a walk outside?" she asked Jeff. "Ralph is a keen gardener, and he's designed one of the most spectacular backyards in California."

"I'd love that," Jeff said, politely clearing a path for her through the crowds, and entertaining her with a droll account of his life reporting in the madhouse of national politics.

"We journalists are a naive bunch at heart," Ariel said, laughing at one of his anecdotes. "We're probably the only people left in America who think that politics and politicians really matter."

He chuckled. "You're right. Anyway, let's talk about you for a while. Tell me about your current project. You're still with PBS, right?"

"Right." She briefly explained about her work with the executive director of the Protect the Whales Foundation. With his help, she'd managed to film the illegal slaughter of an entire pod of whales by renegade Norwegian and Japanese fishermen. Now she was putting together a one-hour special, questioning the official count of the overall whale population. Jeff was clearly fascinated, and peppered her with questions as they skirted the crowded swimming pool and wandered down a path that led toward an arbor of bougainvillea.

"What are you doing in L.A.?" she asked as they progressed farther from the noisy party and deeper into the coolness of the garden. "Is this a business trip?"

Jeff grimaced. "Not really. Unfortunately, I'm deep into a custody battle with my ex-wife. She's mad as hell that we split, and she's determined to punish me. So she's picked the kids as a surefire way to get me steaming."

"Divorce is always horrible, but children make everything even more difficult," Ariel said.

"You're so right." Jeff looked at her as if she'd said something amazingly insightful instead of boringly trite. "My ex-wife, Betsy, wants to come back to L.A. so that she can be close to her mother, although when we were married, she was barely on speaking terms with the woman. Now, suddenly, I'm supposed to believe they're bosom buddies? I don't think so, and I sure don't think my kids need to live in California. In my opinion, they should stay in Washington, where they're happy with their schools, and we can get to see one another every week. Hell, I'm their father. I should count for something in their lives."

"I'm sure the judge will take your feelings into account," Ariel said, unable to suppress a faint internal sigh. Six months ago, she'd turned thirty-three. Overnight, Miranda had developed the obsessional fervor of a Victorian matron in the cause of getting her sister to the altar. Unfortunately, Miranda's choice of potential mates for her sister seemed to consist exclusively of recently divorced men. Jeff was simply the latest in a long list of suffering ex-husbands that Miranda had sent her way.

"God, I hope you're right." Jeff chewed anxiously on his lower lip. "When I was married, the kids drove me crazy with their noise. Now they're gone, the silence is damn near unbearable. I even put on one of their god-awful CDs the other day, just so the apartment wouldn't feel so empty."

He looked so desolate that Ariel found herself responding with genuine concern. "I'm sure the judge will understand that your job keeps you in Washington, and will rule accordingly. The father's needs have a lot more influence on custody arrangements these days, you know."

Jeff's eyes brightened. "Do you really think so?"

"Yes, I do." After all the blind dates Miranda sent her way, Ariel was better informed than she wanted to be on the subject of divorce and child custody. She listened resignedly as Jeff launched into a heartbreaking story about his daughter's recent ballet recital, and how his ex-wife had conspired to make sure that he didn't attend. His daughter was now refusing to speak to him, and he couldn't defend himself without accusing his ex-wife of being a manipulative liar.

"Which is exactly what she is," he concluded bitterly. "That's half the reason I divorced her. I swear to God, she doesn't know the meaning of the word *honest*."

Ariel was much too smart to ask about Jeff's other reasons for divorcing Betsy. She made soothing noises, which was all he really wanted from her, while he recited his litany of com-

plaints. Eventually, he ran out of steam and fell into an embarrassed silence. Apparently disconcerted by his own
behavior, he tugged at his tie, and avoided her eyes as he
apologized.

"My God, I don't usually run on like that. You should have
stopped me," he said. "I was being a royal pain in the ass. And
I'd been so looking forward to meeting you."

"You had a lot on your mind," Ariel said. "Better to get it
off."

As she'd expected, having convinced himself that he'd
made a fool of himself, Jeff was now desperate to find some
excuse to escape her company. She took pity on him, and
provided him with a perfect out.

"Oh, look!" she said, gesturing vaguely into the distance.
"I think I can see Ralph Dunnett at last. Would you excuse
me, Jeff? Ralph's been leaving messages on my answering
machine for the past two days and I really do need to speak
with him."

"Of course, I understand." Jeff barely managed to conceal
his relief at the chance to get away. "It's been nice meeting
you," he said.

"It's been great." Ariel smiled. "See you around, Jeff."

They parted almost at a run. Ariel really had spotted her
brother-in-law, and she managed to connect with him just as
he was scurrying back into the house, looking like a hunted
crab.

"Lovely party, Ralph," she said, trying to sound sincere.

He ran his fingers through his thinning hair and gazed at
her in reproach. "If I wanted to bet on a sure thing, Ariel, I'd
bet that you're hating every minute of this. It's one of the
things I like best about you—your dislike of huge collections
of people gathering together to make horses' rear ends out of
themselves."

She laughed ruefully. "Okay, Ralph, I admit this is close to my definition of torment."

"Mine, too." He shoved his hands into the pockets of his crumpled pants, and rocked back on his heels. "I wonder why I'm so deeply in love with Miranda when we have almost nothing in common."

Over the past year, she and Ralph had become good friends, but this was the first time he'd ever made any reference to his feelings for Miranda. In fact, Ariel had often wondered if he'd married her as some sort of trophy, a young and stunningly beautiful bride to complement his huge fortune.

The gaze Ralph turned on her was uncomfortably shrewd, and she flushed, avoiding his gaze. She was always uncomfortable with any mention of the word *love*. Her parents, who dropped out of mainstream society in the sixties, and forgot to drop back in, used the word so frequently that it had lost its meaning for her long before she was a teenager. Love and peace, brothers and sisters. Sure, why not? Loving strangers was a heck of a lot easier than holding down a job and making sure your kids got fed on time.

"You left a couple of phone messages for me," she said, deliberately changing the subject. "I tried to call you back, but your secretary was in one of her dragon moods and wouldn't put me through."

"We were buying an airline," he said, in the absentminded tone of voice most people would use to mention the purchase of a new screwdriver. "But I do need to talk with you. Could you make lunch next week? Maybe Tuesday?"

She made a quick mental review of her calendar. "Tuesday's fine," she said. "Noon? But somewhere near Beverly Hills, if that's possible. That's where I'll be."

"The Biscayne," he said. "Do you know it?"

Before she could answer, he ducked as if to avoid a blow. "Gigi Harris!" he hissed. "Heading right for us! Take cover!" He scuttled into the safety of the house, leaving her to fend for herself.

No more anxious than Ralph to encounter the notorious gossip columnist, Ariel picked a corner of the garden protected by shrubbery and headed for it at a fast clip, avoiding the few small clusters of guests this far from the main party, and feeling relieved when she didn't encounter anyone she knew. The grounds were huge, but well lit with fairy lights strung in the trees and around the bushes, and she relished the rare chance to be alone in such beautiful surroundings.

She made her way to the wall that circled the perimeter of the property and leaned against the stones, still warm with the day's sunshine. She listened to the distant throb of dance music interspersed with the pounding of the surf on the beach below and gulped in refreshing lungfuls of sea-scented air. There was almost nothing about Miranda's million-dollar life-style that she envied, except this: the smell of the sea, the rocky stretch of private beach and the endless vista of waves crashing onto the deserted and pristine shore.

A sudden gust of cold wind reminded her that it was October, and nights could be chilly. She clutched her witch's hat, catching it just in time to prevent it from sailing off into the ocean. Since it belonged to the TV station, she'd better not lose it.

As quickly as the breeze had sprung up, it died away again, leaving her corner of the garden undisturbed.

Except that she wasn't alone anymore, Ariel realized, resentful that her solitude had been interrupted. A guest, either lost or drunk or both, seemed to materialize out of the center of a clump of oleander bushes that grew to her left, against the wall. He pushed the branches apart, pulling dark green leaves out of his hair as he looked around him with a decidedly furtive air.

Startled by his unexpected appearance, she didn't have the wit to make good her escape before he could corner her, although he definitely looked like the type of obnoxious macho man she would pay money to avoid.

He'd gotten into the spirit of the Halloween festivities by coloring his shoulder-length hair with an iridescent silver spray, and covering his muscled body with silver makeup. Lots of silver makeup that glistened in the moonlight and had been carefully matched to the exact shade of his hair. Smothering a giggle, Ariel decided that he looked like a cross between the Tin Man and Conan the Barbarian.

Good God! Her eyes popped when he stepped out onto the pathway and she registered the astonishing truth. The guy was naked, stark naked, except for his layer of silver body paint.

Ariel blinked, gulped and stared again. She hadn't been mistaken. The silver paint covered every portion of his anatomy, including the parts that proved him to be an exceptionally well-endowed male—much more Conan than Tin Man, that was for sure.

His only concessions toward a costume, other than copious quantities of silver body-paint, were a short shiny stick that was tucked into a decorative belt around his waist, and a narrow metallic chain worn around his neck, from which he'd suspended some sort of holographic laser device that swirled and spun with hidden fire, a vibrant splash of shifting scarlet on his monochrome body.

He seemed to be having second thoughts about his exotic costume—or non-costume. He slunk along the path at a fast clip, darting from bush to bush as if trying to hide, although to Ariel his movements seemed secretive rather than embarrassed. As she watched him approach, she made a quick mental review of various sci-fi movies and TV shows. Who the heck was he supposed to be? An alien from *Star Trek? Babylon Five? Deep Space Nine?* No famous character sprang to mind. Presumably, he was simply an exhibitionist who'd decided to treat the female guests to a display of his attributes—which were admittedly splendid, even if silver body-paint would never have been Ariel's chosen outfit for enhancing the well-developed male anatomy.

She was sorely tempted to flee the scene and leave him to his fate. Then, sisterly feelings got the better of her; she decided she'd be doing Miranda a favor if she kept this weirdo well away from the rest of the guests. He would undoubtedly cause a lot of excited gossip, but even at a Hollywood party, full-frontal nudity wasn't considered good form. And this guy's nudity was very full and very frontal.

With her gaze fixed determinedly on the man's profile, and away from more intimate areas, she stepped out onto the pathway, cutting him off at an angle, but maintaining a safe distance. The guy's muscles looked impressively functional, even if they were painted silver.

"May I help you?" she asked with as much politeness as she could muster. Which at this point wasn't very much. "Perhaps I could steer you in the direction of some clothing?" She didn't attempt to hide her sarcasm.

He jumped at the sight of her, and Ariel realized that a bend in the perimeter wall had kept her hidden from his view. He stared long and hard at her witch's hat, perhaps because he couldn't believe her lack of originality in choosing a costume. He made no comment, however, simply touched his right hand to his left shoulder and spoke in a low, hesitant voice.

"I...thank...you, madame. I...need...no help. Goodbye, madame."

The guy's foreign accent was so badly faked, Ariel wasn't sure whether to laugh or groan. She had no time to debate the problem. One moment she and the man were alone on the pathway. A split second later, a silver-painted woman, equally naked as the man, sprang out of the bushes and threw herself into his outstretched arms.

Gee whiz, a matched pair, Ariel thought in horrified amusement. If it had been anyone else's party, she'd have taken off in double-quick time. Since it was Miranda's, she hesitated for a crucial moment. Just long enough to realize that the couple were not indulging in exuberant sexual foreplay as she'd assumed—they were fighting. And it looked as if they were fighting in deadly earnest.

"Get out of the way!" the woman ordered Ariel, in perfectly normal English. At least she had the sense not to try to fake an alien accent as her silver-haired partner had.

Ariel obeyed, but only because she was trying to decide how best to break up the couple's fight without getting socked on the jaw by a misplaced punch. She was about to take her chances and walk between them, when she saw the gleaming blade of a dagger flash in the woman's hand.

"Hey, quit! Stop that!" Ariel yelled, horrified. "Are you crazy? You're going to hurt each other! Give me the damn knife!"

Both man and woman totally ignored her. Ariel tried to decide whether to run for help, or scream and hope someone would hear her. On the point of running, she saw the man break loose from the woman's arm lock. He stepped back and aimed his stick at her midsection.

Not surprisingly, nothing happened, but the man seemed astonished. For a second, he glanced down at the stick, almost as if he'd forgotten it was part of his costume and expected it to spurt bullets.

The woman laughed, a low, triumphant sound, and closed in, taking advantage of the man's infinitesimal distraction to slash her knife with vicious force all the way down his face and the center of his body. The knife made a sound like chalk scraping on a blackboard, and Ariel sucked in an appalled breath, expecting to see the man's face split open and blood gush all over the gravel pathway.

No wound opened anywhere on his body. In fact, once again nothing happened, except that the couple continued their grim struggle. Not a single speck of blood appeared, and the silver body-paint on the man's arm wasn't even scratched. Far from being injured, the man looked as if he was beginning to win the fight, despite the fact that he was unarmed, and that the woman was clearly trained in hand-to-hand combat.

Ariel finally realized what was going on, and looked around for the cameras. A movie shoot. This had to be a movie shoot. What a crazy place to be filming, she thought. And why the heck hadn't Miranda mentioned anything about a film crew coming to the party? Come to that, why hadn't the director yelled at her to get out of the way?

The man and woman had been wrestling in virtual silence, but the scene was finally winding down. The woman gave a convincing cry of pain. The man grunted with satisfaction and grabbed her hand, dragging her over to the wall, scraping her heels over the path. With apparently brutal force, he smashed her wrist against the stones, and her fingers flew open, releasing the knife. It clattered to the ground at Ariel's feet and, reacting without thought, she bent to pick it up.

The knife was oddly hot to the touch but, as she'd expected, it was clearly a fake, made of silver-colored plastic and light as the proverbial feather. The man called out something, but Ariel couldn't understand what he said, although she had a strange feeling he'd issued some kind of warning.

"What did you say?" she demanded.

She should have saved her breath. He didn't reply, not even with a grunt. His attention was focused on the woman. He wrapped her hair around his fist and pulled her backward, bending her over the wall, his arm pressed against her throat, and his knee shoved into her groin, pinning her in place. Despite their nakedness, there was nothing even remotely sexual about the close physical contact. It seemed to Ariel that the man's entire body was taut with rage and the threat of more violence.

She looked around, searching hard for any glimpse of a camera. Nothing. She looked down at the knife, quelling a sudden terrified lurch of her stomach. It *was* a fake, wasn't it? A stunt prop, the kind that was designed to look lethal but inflict no harm. She ran her thumb along the rim where the plastic blade joined the handle, feeling for the spring mechanism that would allow the blade to retract.

As far as she could determine, there was no such mechanism. She turned the knife over, testing the blade against her thumb. The knife instantly cut so deep that she didn't feel the pain, didn't even realize she'd been wounded, until she saw the blood gush out of her thumb in a bright red spurt.

She stared at the blood, not quite able to believe her own eyes. How could plastic possibly inflict such a deep cut at the mere touch of the blade against her skin? She was still staring at her wounded thumb when the knife was ripped from her grasp by the man.

"It is dangerous," he said. "Do not touch."

The woman murmured something that Ariel couldn't understand. The man pressed the knife against the woman's throat, but she simply laughed defiantly. The point of the blade—which had cut Ariel's thumb at a mere touch—didn't leave a mark on the layer of silver body-paint.

Perhaps the man wasn't really pressing the knife to the woman's throat, Ariel thought, although his attack looked serious enough. With a grunt of effort, he twisted the woman around and threw her to the ground, straddling her, and holding her hands captive above her head with one hand. He poised the knife with hideous menace over her left eye, and this time Ariel was chillingly certain the threat was genuine.

The woman obviously thought so, too. She said something that sounded like, "You win, Robbie."

Robbie—if that was the silver hunk's name—didn't reply. With a swiftness that made it impossible to see exactly how he did it, the man whipped the knife blade straight down the center of her face, then ripped sharply sideways with both hands.

Ariel gave a cry, expecting to see the woman's face sliced in two. Instead, she saw that the silver paint covering the woman's face had popped open, and the man had peeled it off, leaving it crumpled around her shoulders like a sticky, discarded layer of colored Saran Wrap. With the silver covering gone, the woman's face was a perfectly normal light brown color.

Ariel drew in a quick, hard breath. She realized that she felt sick, and that her knees were shaking so much she could barely stand. She didn't understand what was happening, and she was scared. The man still straddled the woman, with the knife now poised at her newly bared throat. Ariel had the sudden terrible conviction that he was going to kill her.

"Don't," she said. "Oh my God, please don't."

Robbie—of course—ignored her. He spoke again to the woman, his eyes riveted on her face. The woman didn't risk moving with that lethal knife held to her throat, but she did laugh and Ariel could have sworn the sound was mocking.

"Surely you don't expect me to give you my transporter coordinates, Robbie," she said.

Ariel was trying to make sense of that cryptic remark when, to her vast relief, she heard the sound of voices and laughter, distant but coming nearer. She reacted by screaming at the top of her lungs, hitching up her long skirt and running as fast as she could toward the sounds. Until she heard normal everyday people talking, she hadn't realized how profoundly scared she was, how totally terrified.

Attracted by her screams, a pair of panting blue and pink rabbits arrived, closely followed by a devil and an angel.

"Wassa matter, honey?" Blue Rabbit was anything but sober, but he looked kindly enough beneath his acrylic fur and foam-rubber ears.

She pointed.

"Oh my God!" he said.

He sounded even more horrified than she would have expected. Ariel swung around, just in time to see Silver Woman jerk her head to one side. The knife the man was holding ran across her throat, leaving a hideous gaping wound.

For an instant, nobody moved. Then the devil and the blue rabbit threw themselves on Silver Hunk, hauling him away from his victim, and restraining him with a punishing, albeit drunken, grip on either side.

The angel knelt beside the wounded woman.

"I'm a doctor," she said, ripping at the hem of her dress and forming a makeshift pad, which she pressed into the gushing wound. "You're going to be fine," she said, her voice shaking a little at the lie. "Sherry, call Emergency Services. And send someone to get my medical kit—"

The doctor continued issuing instructions, but Ariel heard nothing more. With almost laughable ease, Silver Hunk threw off the drunken restraint of the rabbit and the devil, and sprang toward her. In a single fluid movement, he scooped up the knife, which nobody had thought to take charge of, and immobilized Ariel in a chokehold.

"Do . . . not . . . move or I . . . shall . . . kill . . . you," he said, holding the knife a millimeter from Ariel's carotid artery. "You have seen . . . this knife and you know it is capable of killing at my touch."

The devil made an instinctive move to rescue her. Blue Rabbit pulled him back. The Silver Man swung Ariel up into his arms with about as much effort as if she'd been a newborn baby, instead of a hundred-and-thirty-pound, five-foot-seven-inch woman.

Pushing past the devil and Blue Rabbit, he took off toward the wall at a fast headlong run.

Ariel screamed, but no sounds came out. She was so frightened all the breath seemed to have squeezed out of her lungs. The man's skin felt smooth, almost silky, without a trace of sweat, and faintly chill to the touch. The perimeter wall loomed ahead of them, about four feet high at its lowest point.

She closed her eyes in despair. "Don't jump," she croaked. "There's a cliff. Rocks. Ocean currents."

Silver Man barely paused in his stride. He swung sideways and vaulted over the wall, leaping into space with Ariel still in his arms.

She knew that she was about to die. Miranda and Ralph had never needed to build high security fences around their garden because the cliff on the other side of the wall presented a thirty-foot perpendicular drop into the Pacific Ocean.

The man's jump had been far too high and wide for them to land on an outcropping. Air whooshed past as they plummeted through space toward certain death. Ariel's life didn't flash before her eyes. Instead, she found herself wishing she'd had a chance to say goodbye to her sister. And her parents.

How crazy that she'd been too proud to seek a reconciliation with them. What a waste of pride!

An instant before they hit water, she felt Silver Man crush her against his body, his hands cradling her head against his chest.

"Hold your breath!" he commanded. "We shall hit the sea—now!"

The waters of the Pacific closed over her, crushing her lungs.

She gagged on mouthfuls of salty water.

A great weight pressed down on her breast.

Darkness.

2

ARIEL PUSHED slowly out of the enveloping darkness and decided that she hurt far too much to be dead. The sun burned her dry skin, while a gusty breeze left her shivering, her teeth clattering together with the cold. Her body ached everywhere—not just bones and muscles, but fingernails, toenails and the roots of her hair.

She tried to slide back into the comfort of unconsciousness, but her body refused to cooperate. Sighing, she debated the relative merits of opening her eyes, or trying to sit up. Between the thumping pain in her head, and the excruciating pressure on her lungs each time she drew breath, she was quite sure she couldn't manage both.

She compromised by rolling her aching head to the side, and pushing herself up on one elbow before peeling apart her sticky eyelashes.

The view that met her bleary gaze was beautiful, but not promising in terms of rescue. She was lying on a stretch of deserted sandy beach, sheltered from the sun and wind only by a forbidding overhang of sandstone cliffs. Her lips were cracked, her skin crusted with salt, and she was wearing nothing but her bra and her wispy lace panties, a fact that would have embarrassed her more if she'd hadn't felt too battered to worry about modesty.

The soggy remains of what had once been her favorite black evening dress lay in a makeshift cushion beneath her head, and she was so thirsty she would have given her next year's salary for a tall glass of ice water. From the quality of the light, she guessed it was barely past dawn, which meant that she'd been unconscious, or sleeping, for six or seven hours.

The pale November sun lacked heat. Rubbing the goose bumps on her arms in a vain attempt to get warm, Ariel scanned the shore, looking for Robbie, her kidnapper. Not surprisingly, there was no sign of him. It was miracle enough that she'd survived and been washed up onto this little spit of sand; it would be beyond miraculous if he, too, had survived his suicidal leap over the garden wall into the sea.

Still, her gaze flew again to the ocean, searching for a glimpse of him, but the endless roll of white-crested Pacific waves revealed no trace of human life. Which was all to the good, of course, since her current situation would hardly have been improved by finding herself held hostage by a lunatic with powerful muscles, a weird accent and a kinky tendency to walk around naked.

Perversely, she found herself wishing that Robbie had survived. She'd been watching him closely last night—truth to tell, she'd found him mesmerizing—and she was quite sure that he'd slashed the silver-painted woman's throat by accident. The woman had jerked her head, deliberately twisting beneath the lethal blade. Ariel had seen his face clearly as the dagger made contact with the woman's flesh, and she was sure he'd been shocked and horrified by the terrible wound he inflicted.

However, sympathy for her deranged abductor could be saved for later, when she was safely home again. Having grown up in a family where she was the only one who ever thought about boring things like paying the utility bills and doing the laundry, Ariel prided herself on being practical, efficient and strictly no-nonsense in her approach to life. Right now, she needed to work out how she would get herself home. No easy task when she was lacking money, credit cards and identification. Not to mention clothes. Or the faintest clue as to where she was. For all she knew, she could have washed up in Mexico. Or Oregon.

Her brain cells seemed as reluctant to function as the rest of her body, but thirst soon caused her survival instincts to kick in. One step at a time, she told herself. Gritting her teeth, she started on the daunting task of levering her aching body upright.

The moment she put weight on her left leg, she collapsed, toppling flat on her back as sparks of excruciating pain shot out from her toe to her knee. Blinking away tears, Ariel stared at the sky and gave vent to her entire—not very colorful—vocabulary of swearwords. Damn! If her ankle wasn't broken, it was sprained so badly that walking was going to be a major challenge.

"Feeling sorry for yourself will get you nowhere," she muttered. "Now get up and start walking, or crawling, or whatever it takes to haul your stupid carcass off this damn beach."

Taking care not to move her left foot too quickly, she propped her back against the wall of rock and eased herself into a sitting position. The maneuver brought her feet into focus for the first time since she'd regained consciousness, and she stared at her injured ankle in blank astonishment. The lower half of her leg was encased in a makeshift splint, fashioned of pieces of driftwood, bound neatly in place by strips of black satin.

She grabbed her dress and examined the wet skirt. Yep, somebody had cut neat circular strips from the hem, leaving it about eighteen inches shorter than before. Who had found her? And where was her rescuer now?

Probably he, or she, had gone to call for paramedics, Ariel decided. She wished that her rescuer had at least left a note saying, Chin up, back soon! The knowledge that she'd been found once, and then abandoned, made her feel doubly alone.

On the other hand, she might be lucky to have woken before her rescuer returned. God knows, after her experiences the night before with Robbie, she should be taking steps to protect herself from strangers, not waiting for them to return and find her helpless on the beach. There were plenty of crazies around who would be quite capable of tending to her ankle just so that she'd be all in one piece when they cracked open her skull.

Seized by a new sense of urgency, Ariel slung the remains of her dress around her neck, grabbed on to a spar of rock and hauled herself upright. Panting, but triumphant, she tried— with a total lack of success—to shake the wet sand out of her evening dress. Sighing at the inevitable, she pulled the gritty material over her head, and tugged at the zipper, shivering as the clammy fabric tightened around her salt-roughened skin. The thin chiffon sleeves were in tatters and the dress had shrunk so that it clung to every curve and hollow of her body. If she looked even a tenth as bedraggled as she felt, she'd be arrested for vagrancy by the first cop who saw her. Which might not be such a bad thing, Ariel reflected with wry humor. A ride in a nice warm squad car sounded very appealing at this moment.

But there was never a cop around when you needed one, so how was she going to get off the beach? She eyed the rock she was leaning against with dislike. As far as she could see, there was no way to reach civilization without clambering across at least fifteen feet of rugged sandstone. Normally, such a simple climb would have presented no challenge. In her current state, however, Ariel felt as if she'd been asked to scale Mount Everest without benefit of a rope or pitons.

Thirst finally concentrated her scattered wits. Perhaps there would be an easier way off the beach if she walked around the rocks rather than attempted to climb up and over them. Protecting her ankle by clinging to handholds of rock as she hopped forward, Ariel struggled around the rocky barrier, allowing herself a small whoop of triumph when she finally made it to the next cove and saw that her efforts had been rewarded. A pathway wound its way off the sand, climbing between two imposing cliffs, and disappearing into a thick stand of sea pines and gnarled cypress trees. The trees blocked her view, but if there was a path, surely a road and people couldn't be too far away.

On the brink of starting to climb up the path, she halted in her tracks when she saw a man emerge from the trees. Good God, it was Robbie! Carrying a large plastic jug, he strode down the rocky path at an amazingly fast pace, moving as easily as if his bare feet were cushioned by thick rubber soles. She rubbed her eyes, but she wasn't hallucinating. Robbie's silver body covering glowed with undiminished brightness in the dappled sunlight filtering through the trees, and he hadn't bothered to clothe himself, or even to drape a few strategic leaves in a minor concession to public decency.

Ariel was so shocked by the shiny perfection of his body makeup that she almost forgot to be shocked by his nakedness. The layer of iridescent paint shone as brilliantly as it had the night before. Far from appearing injured by his insane leap into the Pacific Ocean, he seemed in the best of health, and bursting with energy. The antithesis of her bedraggled self, in fact. The only change Ariel could see was that his hair was no longer silver. Instead, it was a gleaming shade of ebony, thick and shiny with health.

Why had his body paint survived its immersion in sea-water, when his hair color had completely washed out? Ariel realized suddenly that she found Robbie's silver body-wrap frightening in its perfection. How in the world had he maintained its shiny smoothness after a plunge into the Pacific, and several hours of exposure to sand, sun, wind and salty air?

She didn't wait to ask. She simply turned and ran. Within seconds, her ankle collapsed, and she ended up in an ignominious heap, spitting sand and curses with equal vehemence. She had barely managed to pull herself onto her knees when she felt Robbie's hands reaching for her, lifting her off the ground and cradling her in his arms with surprising gentleness.

"Foolish woman, you will do permanent damage to your ankle," he said, running back toward the cover of the cypress trees. His stride was light, springy and energetic, and he seemed to find her weight no more burdensome than she would have found carrying a kitten.

"Did the splint break?" he asked, sounding worried. "I did not expect you to wake so soon, or I would not have left in search of water. I know you must be dehydrated."

"Put me down!" The remnants of her control snapped and she pummeled his chest, aware that she was hurting her own hands far more than she was hurting Robbie, but unable to deny the panic that overwhelmed her. "Put me down, you crazy idiot! Let me go!"

"I regret that I cannot. Here, drink this water and then we must leave this place at once. I have seen people assembled in the forecourt of a building near here. I believe they are military personnel. I do not wish to speak with military personnel."

"I'll just bet you don't," Ariel muttered, but she took the jug and was about to gulp down a giant, satisfying swallow, when she realized he could have spiked it with any number of harmful things.

She held out the jug, so ravaged by thirst that she was almost willing to drink the water even if he admitted he'd laced it with arsenic. "You drink some first," she said hoarsely.

He didn't say anything, just took the jug and swallowed three or four mouthfuls, then handed it back to her. "It came from a spigot attached to the exterior of a building. It will not harm you, woman. I have checked for bacteria and other contaminants, and the level of pollution is not lethal."

Ariel was too thirsty to care that he was talking nonsense. Checked for contaminants, my foot! Still, if he could drink the water, so could she. She tipped the jug to her mouth and let the water chug down her throat in a glorious stream. It was tepid, but she didn't care; it tasted wonderful, magnificent, the best water she'd ever had in her life. She drew in a deep breath, then drank again, splashing the final few drops over her face, washing away some of the dried salt.

Robbie barely waited for her to finish drinking before he broke into a run, jogging up the path toward the trees.

Ariel's fighting spirit revived now that she was no longer fixated on her need for water. She might have a damaged ankle, she reflected, but at least mentally she was more or less normal. Which had to give her an advantage over Silver Hunk, whose wits—to put it politely—appeared somewhat addled.

"Where are you taking me?" she asked, wondering if he actually had some sort of lunatic, cockeyed plan, or if he was simply running at random.

"We are going north," he said.

"Any special reason why we're going north?"

He looked down at her as if the answer should be obvious. "Because we were carried 24.62 kilometers south by the currents of the Pacific Ocean and we both need to return to the neighborhood where we entered the water."

We were carried 24.62 kilometers south. Yeah, right. It was just possible that Robbie knew which direction the ocean currents had taken them. There was no way in the world he could know precisely how far they'd been carried, unless he'd seen a signpost indicating where they were. And why would a signpost be marked in kilometers rather than miles? His claim was patent nonsense, and yet, for some odd reason, Ariel couldn't quite bring herself to dismiss it.

"How can you possibly know exactly what distance we traveled?" she asked. "Or even what direction?"

He hesitated. "It is complicated," he said. "But I am quite sure we ended up on a beach that was 24.62 kilometers south of the point where we entered the water. You can accept my word on this, woman."

Ariel counted to ten, warning herself not to frighten him by disputing his claims. The guy was indisputably nuts, and Lord knew what he might do if she spooked him. Next time she asked her guardian angel to send her an exciting man, she promised herself she'd do a better job of defining *exciting*.

On the other hand, if by any wild chance Robbie happened to be accurate in his claims, Ariel guessed they must have washed up somewhere on the shores of Camp Pendleton, which would at least explain why the beaches were so deserted. Camp Pendleton was a giant Marine Corps base that covered more than a hundred and fifty square miles of potentially prime real estate south of L.A. and north of San Diego. The marines used some of the more isolated beaches to stage mock battles, and these combat beaches were off limits to the public.

At this moment, Ariel would have been real happy to see a few dozen marines in combat gear swarming onto the sand to practice their assault landings. Unfortunately, this didn't seem to be a day for war games. There wasn't a marine in sight. In fact, other than Robbie, there didn't seem to be another human being in sight.

Not that she could see very much. Robbie was holding her face pressed against his chest, almost as if he were trying to cushion her from being jostled as he ran, but Ariel realized that must be an illusion. Why would he care about her comfort? She was his prisoner, and, in truth, she had very little hope of escape, given her sprained ankle and the generally battered state of her body. Not to mention the inconvenient fact that Robbie's mental abilities might be on the low side, but he seemed physically fit enough to give any superhero a run for his money.

His skin felt abnormally cool against her wind-burned cheek, as if the layer of silver that covered him prevented the escape of body heat. Ariel shivered, and not only because of the chilly breeze. She was beginning to think thoughts about Mr. Robbie Silver Hunk that scared her. Like maybe she'd fallen into the ocean and woken up in the Twilight Zone. Or a planet orbiting a distant star. Why else did she keep sneaking glances to see if she could spot a spaceship hovering on top of one of the cypress trees?

Get a grip, girl, she told herself. Aliens in silver space suits do not land in people's backyards except on TV and at the movies.

"You'd travel much faster without me," she suggested, hoping against hope that he would listen. "Honestly, Robbie, there's no sense in taking me with you, wherever you're going. I'm just slowing you down."

"It is true that you slow my pace, by approximately 17.5 percent, but you need medical attention. And since it is my fault that you were injured, I am obligated to return you to your housing unit, or at least to a place of safety in your neighborhood."

"I'll be fine if you leave me here, Robbie. Honest. Look, there's a bunch of buildings right over there, on the far side of the trees. Drop me off right here."

"I am well aware of the buildings. Unfortunately, I cannot risk having you inform the authorities that we have survived, therefore I cannot take the risk of setting you free until our escape route has been secured."

"Wh-what does that mean?"

"Nothing that need alarm you. You have nothing to fear from me, woman. It has never been my intention to harm you in any way. It is my sincere wish to protect you."

She wished she could believe him. "If you really mean what you say, Robbie, the quickest way to get me the medical attention I need is to let me go. Right here. Now. I'll turn myself in to the first marine I see and you can be on your way."

"Marine?" He repeated the word, as if testing it out, but he didn't slacken his pace even for a moment, much less turn inland, toward the buildings now distantly visible through the trees.

"Yes, you know, one of those military personnel you saw when you went looking for water. I think we've ended up on the Marine Corps base at Camp Pendleton."

"Marines," he said again, a note of something akin to wonder in his voice. "The army, the navy, the air force and the marines. We are on a marine base."

He looked lost in thought, as if he were contemplating something quite extraordinary. Ariel swallowed hard, fighting to untangle the knot tying itself in her stomach. She heard the sound of a car engine starting up, and almost cried with relief at the everyday familiarity of the noise. She hated this feeling of having woken up in Wonderland.

"Set me free," she pleaded. "Robbie, let me go and I won't say anything about having seen you, I promise. I'll tell everyone I found my own way off the beach and that I've no idea what happened to you. In fact, I won't even mention you, how's that for a deal?"

"It is incredible." He looked down at her, and his mouth quirked into a surprising smile. "And if I believe that promise, woman, you also have a bridge in Brooklyn you would like to sell to me, is that not so?"

It was the first time he'd said anything that indicated he had even a marginal sense of humor. She discovered that his voice had a warm, husky note that was oddly appealing. She licked her painfully cracked lips. "I don't have any bridges to sell, Robbie. No deals I'm trying to pull. I just want to go home. Please let me go."

He hesitated for a moment. "I regret that it is not possible to grant your request. The truth is, you are in too much danger for me to let you go. But if you tell me where you live, woman, I will take you there as quickly as possible. Then, when I have made the necessary arrangements for your safety, I will disappear from your life."

Right, sure he would. And would he murder her before or after he raped her?

He slowed his pace, finally coming to a complete halt. His dark blue eyes stared down at her with disconcerting understanding. "Your thoughts are written on your face, woman. But you should learn to trust me. I will not hurt you, I give you my word."

She grimaced ruefully. "And if I believe that, Robbie, you have a bridge in Brooklyn you'd like to sell me, right?"

It was crazy to provoke him, even crazier to assume he would be amused by the fact that she was repeating his own wry comment back to him, but he actually laughed, a quick chuckle that ended almost as soon as it began. Then his expression sobered and he drew more deeply into the cover provided by a stand of overgrown cypress trees. Ariel had the distinct impression that he was wrestling with some sort of internal debate.

"My name is Robert Macmillan," he said finally. "I was born in . . . Canada. My friends do not call me Robbie. They call me Mac. I would be honored if you, too, would call me Mac."

Robert Macmillan. It sounded like a very ordinary name for a most unusual man. And why did he want to be addressed as Mac, when the woman last night had called him Robbie? Better not to ask him about the events of last night, Ariel decided. For all she knew, Mr. Robert Macmillan might turn into a gibbering lunatic at the first mention of the woman whose throat he'd slit. Better to placate him while she had the chance.

"My name's Ariel Hutton," she said, and immediately wondered why in the world she'd given him her correct name. "It's . . . um . . . it's nice to meet you, Mac."

He bowed his head in a formal gesture that should have looked absurd, but didn't. "I am honored by the gift of your name." He shifted slightly, adjusting the weight of her body in his arms. The movement brought her head higher on his shoulder and rubbed her breast against the solid wall of his chest. He glanced down at her, his expression arrested, and Ariel was suddenly acutely reminded of the fact that—beneath his layer of silver—Mac was naked.

"I'm too heavy for you to carry," she said quickly. "Why don't you put me down. Please, Mac?"

"You are not heavy," he said. His brilliant blue eyes, an unusual contrast to his black hair, met her gaze unsmilingly. "It is not my arms that hold you prisoner, Ariel, but your ankle. You could not run more than two or three steps before I caught you, or before you did yourself a major and serious injury."

"Why do you need to catch me?" she asked. "If you stop and think for a minute, you'll realize I'm no danger to you. You run so fast that by the time I found a marine, or a police officer, you would be miles away from here."

"I cannot allow you to speak of our survival to the police," he said. "It is important that your government authorities believe us to be dead. But there is another reason why I cannot let you go. I am in desperate need of a friend, and it is my great hope that you will become that friend. Is that possible, Ariel? Will you help me?"

How did she do it? Ariel asked herself. How was it that every lame duck and weirdo in the state always managed to make a beeline for her? Why did men develop this neurotic compulsion to pour out their crazy, ridiculous problems into her totally unsympathetic ears? How come nobody ever seemed to notice that she was the practical, sensible member of her family? It was her parents and sister who were eccentric, creative, off-the-wall and accepting. She was dull, plodding, boring Ariel. And happy to be that way. Which was only one of the reasons that made it downright silly for her to be feeling a glow of pleasure because Mac, who last night had taken her hostage, this morning claimed to have chosen her for his friend.

She spoke determinedly. "Mac, I'm not the right person to help you. I'm very busy with my own problems right now and I don't have the time or the patience to—"

"You may not yet realize it, Ariel, but at this moment your problems are mine. You need my help, as I need yours."

"I don't think so—"

"I wish to ask you some questions, that is all."

"What sort of questions?"

"A very simple one, to begin with. What date is it today?"

"The date?" Ariel blinked. "You want to know today's date?"

"If you please." She could sense the tension radiating through him as he waited for her answer.

"November first," she replied cautiously. He showed no reaction, so she risked elaborating a little. "It was Halloween last night, remember? October thirty-first."

"Halloween." He said the word as he had said *marine*, making it sound like an unfamiliar ingredient in an exotic recipe. Then suddenly he smiled. "Well, at least that explains the doctor escorted by blue and pink rabbits! However hard I tried, I could find no explanation for that!"

If he'd forgotten last night was Halloween, then why had he slathered himself in silver body paint, and turned up at her sister's party naked? She looked away from his smile, all her old doubts returning. She considered the unpleasant fact that somebody who was totally disconnected from reality might be a lot more dangerous than a guy who simply wasn't very smart.

Mac put his hand under her chin and gently pulled her head around so that she was looking straight at him. "Before you worry yourself into total silence, Ariel, I have another question for you, if you please. I need to know what year it is."

"The year? You need to know the year?" Ariel suddenly realized what had happened. Good grief, of course! Mac was suffering from amnesia! Why hadn't she thought of that before?

"Oh my God, did you hit your head on a rock when you jumped into the sea? Mac, you need to go to the hospital. You probably have a concussion—"

"The date," he said harshly. "What year is it, Ariel? I don't have amnesia, but I . . . very much . . . need to know."

"It's 1996," she said curtly. "It's 1996, Mac."

"It's 1996," he repeated blankly.

"Yep. All year long."

"My God!" he muttered, staring at the office buildings beyond the trees. "It's November first, 1996."

What was bothering him, Ariel wondered. The fact that it was November, or the fact that it was 1996? Had he escaped from a lunatic asylum and just now realized he'd been locked up for years and years? Or was he worried because he'd missed some important engagement on October thirty-first?

She sounded clipped and angry when she spoke, because she was nervous and her throat seemed to be closing up on her. "We're in November, Mac, which means you've had ten months to get used to the idea that this is 1996. Just over four years until we hit the second millennium. Bill Clinton is president of the United States, *Forrest Gump* won last year's Oscar for Best Movie and the good ole' baseball players have managed to play an entire season without going on strike. Does this ring any bells, Mac?"

"Faint ones," he said. "At least the part about President Clinton." He shook his head, and gave a tiny, almost imperceptible grin. "My parents always told me I should pay more attention to my history lessons in school."

History lessons? That's it, Ariel decided. The guy was clearly several bricks short of a full load. She had to believe that he was mad—because the alternative was to accept that she herself was crazy.

The revving of the car engine had long since faded into the distance, and in the ensuing silence the caw of a sea gull sounded very loud. But she couldn't hear Mac breathing, Ariel realized, and his heartbeat was imperceptible, even though she was pressed tight against his body. Not a trace of sweat, not a degree of heat exuded from his body, despite the fact that he'd just carried her the best part of three miles, running barefoot all the way.

She rubbed her hand over the silver film covering his body. "What do you have covering you, Mac? What's this silver stuff really made of? Obviously, it isn't makeup." She realized she should have asked the question long ago, and she was trembling as she waited for his answer. "Why didn't the silver coating on your skin wash off in the ocean, Mac? The color in your hair all came out."

"My skin covering didn't wash off in the ocean because it is designed to be unaffected by water and other everyday elements, in order to protect the wearer," he said. "It is a biochemically engineered product that has been popular in my world for almost a quarter of a century. We call it permapel. It is able to maintain the body temperature of the wearer at a comfortable level, and it cannot be penetrated except by a libidium blade inserted at precisely the correct angle."

"Libidium?"

He gestured to the knife he'd used to slash the woman's throat the night before—a lifetime ago. "This is made of libidium. As you discovered when you touched it, libidium can be honed to lethal sharpness."

Ariel wanted to laugh at his nonsense, but discovered that she couldn't. Her voice was somewhere between a squeak and a whisper when she finally managed to speak. "I've never heard of anything called permapel," she said. "Or libidium."

Mac was silent for a moment. "That is because neither substance exists in your world," he said, watching her closely. "But they are extensively manufactured in mine."

Her heart was pounding and her pulse was jumping nervously. "Your world, my world. We're both in the same place, the same world." She swallowed hard over the lump in her throat. "You're not making too much sense, Mac."

He looked straight into her eyes. She found it disconcerting that his gaze seemed so intelligent, so entirely sane. "We come from the same world, Ariel, but not from the same time. Permapel is a product from my time, not yours, as is libidium." His hands stroked absently against her arms, almost as if he was soothing her. "In my country—in my time—

we wear permapel instead of clothes, and we use different colors and patterns to mark different stages or events in our lives."

"Wh-what does the color silver mean?" Crazy, lunatic question. Surely she didn't believe his nonsense about permapel and living in a different time, did she?

Mac's answer came slowly. She couldn't decide whether he was inventing his response, or whether he was simply reluctant to convey the information. "Silver is the color traditionally reserved for a very special occasion—the day when a man and a woman celebrate the fact that they are licensed to become parents."

Ariel wondered why she wasn't struggling frantically to get away from the maniac who was holding her, then told herself it was because she was nursing her strength, waiting for a moment when her struggles might have a chance of succeeding. Dawn had given way to early morning, the sun was getting hotter and brighter. Soon, quite soon, she would surely encounter another human being. And that would be the moment to escape. In the meantime, she should try to keep Mac as calm and happy as possible.

"How very interesting," she said politely. "Is that why you're wearing silver, Mac? Because you've been...um... licensed as a parent?"

He smiled, as if he understood perfectly well that she was only pretending to take his answers seriously. "My culture is very different from yours, I realize that, Ariel. In your time, I know that couples need a license to marry, but they need no permission from the social authorities in order to have children. In my time, people are free to enter into sexual relationships whenever they want, but they must put in an application and pass many tests in order to receive the license that permits them to have children."

"Is that so?" she said in the same carefully polite voice. "I daresay, some people might consider that quite a sensible idea, even in my time."

"The majority of our citizens certainly think so," Mac said.

"How do you stop people from having babies before they get their license?" Ariel asked, wondering just how far he'd worked out the practical details of his crazy fantasy world.

"Birth-control devices are implanted in every newborn infant. When two people are approved as potential parents, their implants are removed at a special ceremony, and all their friends throw a big party to celebrate the occasion. The Silver Ceremony, we call it."

She had her answer: his delusion was obviously thought through with care. "How—nice," she said.

"It is much more than nice," Mac said. "It is one of the most important occasions in a person's life. The couple who will become parents wear silver at this ceremony, and it is the only occasion in our lives when we wear this color. Hence, those couples who are preparing to mate are known as Silver Partners. We have many honored traditions and customs associated with the event."

"It sounds like a ch-charming occasion."

He looked down at her, his expression rueful. "You believe that I am crazy, don't you?"

"Well, not exactly crazy." She corrected herself hastily. "No, not at all crazy, in fact. It's just that it's a bit hard to imagine the sort of society you've described—"

"That's because such a society doesn't exist in 1996. In fact, it didn't exist until fifteen years after the Great Famine."

She swallowed hard. "What was the Great Famine, Mac?"

"It was the most important event of the twenty-first century," he said, his eyes darkening. "The Great Famine began in 2043, and in ten terrible years, the world lost nearly two billion people to the ravages of starvation. The suffering was so terrible that civilization was almost wiped out. In the Americas, we were not as badly affected as in parts of Africa and Asia, and so the survivors of the famine joined together across the American continents to create a new country, and a new social order, one that has gradually enabled us to enjoy peace and plenty."

She had to hand it to him, Ariel thought. The guy sure had his delusions carefully worked out. He wasn't trying to put one over on her, she was sure of it. Mac honestly believed what he was saying. He truly thought he was a time traveler. Did that make him more or less dangerous than a run-of-the-mill lunatic? she wondered.

She gave him a smile that she hoped didn't appear too nervous. "All this information about the future is really fascinating, Mac. I'm glad things are going so well for you and that you're all ready for your Silver...um...Ceremony. It's great that you're about to become a father."

There seemed no harm in pretending to believe him. Just so long as he didn't decide she was his designated Silver Partner, chosen by destiny to become the mother of his child. Thank heavens she hadn't been wearing a silver dress last night, or he probably would have raped her hours ago.

Please God, if you could send in a detachment of nice, unimaginative U.S. Marines right about now, I'd consider that a really big favor.

"You believe that I am insane," Mac said. "It is only to be expected. But if you will just accept that I have come back to your time from two hundred years in the future, everything will become quite easy to understand. Consuela Timmons and I were both transported back from Day 214, in the year 2196."

"Consuela Timmons?" she said. "Do you mean the woman who was with you last night?"

"Yes." His voice shook with barely suppressed rage. "Consuela is...was...my chosen Silver Partner. She had agreed to become the mother of my child and then she betrayed me in the most terrible way possible. She is the reason that I have traveled back here to your time."

"T-to kill her?" Ariel asked, then immediately regretted the question. God knows, she didn't want to awaken any latent homicidal impulses.

"Not to kill her," Mac said tightly. "To arrest her."

"Because she ran out on your Silver Ceremony?" Ariel asked.

"No," he said grimly. "Because she committed murder."

Oh, brother. Ariel cleared her throat. "I guess I'm having some trouble understanding the details of your situation, Mac. Why is Consuela here in 1996, if she committed murder in...er...did you say 2196?"

"She could not hope to escape from justice if she remained in our own time," he said, his expression grim. "This was her escape route. I believe she did not expect me to follow her back into the past. When she entered the time-travel chamber, she believed she had escaped the consequences of her crime."

Ariel had a definite feeling that she'd seen the TV movie that formed the basis of Mac's fantasy. Obviously, Mac had watched a few too many reruns. Probably while incarcerated in the state mental institution. "Exactly who did Consuela murder?" she asked.

"She killed her own sister," Mac said.

"That's a terrible thing to have done," Ariel said.

"In our society, it is almost unheard of. We are not a violent people. Since the Great Famine, we have learned to value peace and cooperation. We have crime, and criminals, of course, but not very many. We find that nurturing families and careful education encourage most people to become honest citizens."

"Why were you the person sent back in pursuit of Consuela?" Ariel asked. "Wouldn't it be more logical to send a cop?" Good grief, she thought. I asked those questions as if I thought they were perfectly sensible.

Mac looked puzzled. "A cop?"

"A law enforcement officer. Cop is slang."

"I am a . . . cop." He shrugged, looking almost embarrassed. "In fact, I am the director of the United Bureau of Criminal Investigation. The chief of police for the republic, so to speak."

"Well, imagine that." She couldn't conceal her sarcasm. Obviously, it wasn't enough for him to pretend to be a cop from the twenty-second century, or even a high-ranking detective. No, he had to be the director of the whole damn police bureau, as well. Annoyed that for a split second she'd almost started to believe him, Ariel didn't try to hide her impatience. "I'm surprised you came back to my time in person, Mac. Why didn't send one of your deputies?"

He appeared genuinely astonished by her question. "Consuela committed her crime in front of all our friends, gathered to witness our Silver Ceremony. Even if her victim had been the most humble and anonymous citizen in the Americas, I would have considered myself duty bound to make the arrest. But such is not the case. Consuela's sister, Manuela Timmons, is the president of the United Republic of the Americas and Consuela deliberately exploited the intimate nature of the gathering to assassinate our head of state and make good her escape. After such a betrayal, do you imagine that I could assign the task of arresting her to anyone other than myself?"

Ariel could feel her grasp on reality slipping. "Wait," she said. "Let me make sure I have this straight. Consuela's sister was the president of your country?"

"Yes." Mac sounded almost impatient. "Manuela Timmons had taken the oath of office at the start of her second term only five days ago."

"And now she's dead." Ariel smothered a desire to burst into laughter. Or tears. "So the president of the United Republic of the Americas has been murdered by her sister and you're a time-traveling cop on the trail of the assassin. Who happens to be the woman you'd chosen as the mother of your future children. Have I got that right?"

"In a broad outline, yes. Consuela and I would have been permitted only one child, though, not several."

"Well, now I guess everything makes perfect sense," Ariel said with heavy sarcasm. "I wonder why I didn't think of that explanation, myself?"

"Because human beings in the twentieth century have very limited intelligence," Mac snapped. "Along with feeble and inadequate bodily functions compared to the genetically enhanced strength of people in my time. Now, please tell me where you live so that I can take you home and make arrangements to ensure your safety while I search for Consuela."

She might be a bit punch-drunk, what with one thing and another, but she wasn't yet completely crazy. Obviously, Mac was a psychopathic liar with homicidal tendencies. She would be signing her own death warrant if she gave him the directions to her home. If it was going to be a case of die now, while trying to escape, or die later, after Mac had indulged in an hour or so of torture, she certainly preferred to die now, in the open air, with the sun shining on her face, and birds singing.

Given Mac's physical prowess, there was no realistic hope of escape, of course, but that didn't mean she couldn't try. Ariel pushed against the wall of his chest with every atom of her strength, and screamed for help at the top of her lungs.

"For God's sake, do not make such a noise!" Mac said. "Ariel, stop! If this is truly a military encampment, you will bring the entire Marine Corps running to our sides."

"I sure as hell hope so," she panted between blows.

"I'm sorry, but I cannot permit discovery at this time." His face seemed to take on an oddly regretful expression as she twisted and squirmed in his arms with the desperate strength of the condemned. "Forgive me, Ariel," he said. "I wish there could be another way."

"Wh-what are you going to do?"

"This." His hand pressed against her windpipe. The laser device at his throat pulsed. She felt one short sharp burst of pain, and then there was only the hum of scarlet darkness.

3

SO FAR, Mac thought wryly, he'd handled everything real well. Consuela had escaped, he was undoubtedly wanted by the police for attempted murder and he'd been forced not only to take Ariel captive, but also to render her unconscious. Too many more successes like these, and he should win the Screwup of the Year Award, no problem.

He struggled into the flowered pants and ruffled pink upper garment—he vaguely remembered it was called a shirt—that he'd stolen from some unfortunate citizen's clothesline. The shirt fit okay, but the pants were seriously uncomfortable: too tight at the waist, and bunching uncomfortably in the crotch, but now that he knew how far back in time he'd traveled, he realized he couldn't walk around wearing nothing but permapel. In the twentieth century, honest citizens never appeared in public with their sexual organs exposed, so he had no choice but to put on the damn clothes and suffer. He certainly didn't want to stand out from the crowd, even though he couldn't begin to imagine why people in 1996 found it imperative to cover some of their body parts and not others. Why breasts, he wondered, but not thighs? And if female breasts had to be concealed, why not male nipples? The mysteries of primitive social culture were beyond him.

Ariel's attitude this morning had demonstrated that he had no hope of passing himself off as a visitor from a distant country. Until he familiarized himself with the basic customs of the 1990s—and got rid of his permapel—he would continue to stick out like a sore thumb. And that meant he needed to win Ariel's trust so that she would show him how to blend in with his surroundings.

Without the appropriate solvent, there was no way he could remove the permapel for at least another four hours, at which point, with the aid of some hot water, it would begin to self-destruct. On the plus side, that meant he had another few hours of protection from the hazards of twentieth-century living. Without his layer of permapel, he'd have run a much greater risk of injury when he'd dived into the Pacific and it would have been harder to generate the heat needed to cure Ariel's hypothermia. On the minus side, the permapel made him uniquely conspicuous, an easy target for law enforcement authorities trying to track him.

If only he'd had some warning that he would be traveling back in time, he could have made some preparations, learned how to speak twentieth-century English, brushed up on his knowledge of social history, had himself inoculated and stocked up on his internal supply of healing medications. As it was, he'd been thrust into a life-and-death situation with barely a nanosecond of preparation for the place and time he ended up in.

Still, he'd scanned the area carefully with his Pip, and there didn't seem to be any law officers—cops—in the vicinity. Trouble was, even though he'd finally been able to set the correct date on his Pip, he still couldn't supply the data that would enable Pip to identify law enforcement personnel from this time period, which left Mac uncomfortably vulnerable.

Keeping his head low and his shoulders hunched to conceal as much silver skin as possible, Mac hurried back across the narrow road, his heart racing as he dodged between two automobiles tooling along the bumpy gravel road without a single external safety control to keep them on track. He'd seen demonstrations of primitive transportation systems in museums, of course, but it was one thing to watch a simulation, and another thing altogether to see the mechanical monsters in real life, belching fumes as they roared down the slippery road under the haphazard control of a driver who might, or might not, be paying attention. In some cases, he knew that drivers had actually died at the wheel of their vehicles, and when that happened, there was no automatic locking device to prevent them crashing into whatever barrier happened to be nearest.

Incredible! Mac marveled at the recklessness of his ancestors. Add that recklessness to their basic physical fragility, and he couldn't imagine how enough of his forebears had survived the dangers of their daily lives to create the population explosion that precipitated the Great Famine.

Still, fascinating as it was, he couldn't afford to stand here watching a slice of history unfold in front of him. It was almost eight in the morning, and with every minute that passed, more people were emerging from the single-story housing units. Thank God, the clothes he'd stolen seemed to be providing the disguise he needed, because nobody stopped him or tried to talk with him. It was easy to avoid the few pedestrians by dodging into doorways, or hiding behind shrubbery—this world had so much living foliage!—and the automobile drivers didn't give him a second glance.

He hurried back to the spot where he'd left Ariel sleeping, nestled on a patch of sandy ground, hidden by a stand of cypress. It was an extraordinary sensation to run through a thicket of wild trees, with no nature warden anywhere in sight, and Mac couldn't resist taking a couple of precious seconds to breathe in the sea air, and listen to the noisy caw of sea gulls fighting over a dead fish. God, people in the 1990s didn't know how lucky they were to be surrounded by such natural wonders.

In other circumstances, it would have been deeply rewarding to explore a world in which there were so few people that huge swaths of land could be left almost untouched, their ecosystems uncharted and unprotected. But he had no time to explore now. The need to arrest Consuela was not only an urgent professional duty, it was a personal imperative: a burning goad, twisting painfully in Mac's gut. He knew he had to catch up with her soon, before she wreaked major havoc both in this time and in his own. Consuela might have managed to deceive him about a lot of things, but he knew her well enough to be quite certain that her arrival here at the end of the twentieth century was no accident. She had plotted her escape from the murder scene with meticulous attention to detail, and the time-travel chamber she fled to had been preprogrammed to this precise date in 1996.

That meant Consuela was here for a very specific reason. And the galling truth was that he didn't have a clue what that reason might be. Why 1996, for heaven's sake? Obviously, she planned to take advantage of some historical circumstance to further her own ends. But what circumstance? For the life of him, he couldn't think of any really important social or political event that had occurred in the middle of the 1990s.

Even now, eighteen hours after Consuela's brutal stabbing of her sister, he still couldn't quite grasp the enormity of her betrayal. For the Americas, the loss of President Manuela Timmons was a tragedy that would be hard to overcome. On a personal level, the loss of the woman he'd chosen as his Silver Partner left him feeling raw, his heart bruised and his professional pride pounded into the dust.

The knowledge that Consuela had exploited their relationship to commit the ultimate act of political treachery left him ice-cold with rage. Rage at Consuela for using him, and a worse rage at himself, for being so blind and stupid that he'd never even noticed he was being used. He was the republic's director of security, for God's sake, and with a few loving kisses, a few sentimental whispers about the baby they would soon make together, Consuela had managed to convince him that President Timmons could safely attend their Silver Ceremony with the protection of a single bodyguard. His dereliction of duty stuck in his craw, like a lump of poisoned food that could never be digested.

Forcing himself to put aside the useless recriminations, Mac touched the glowing Pip hanging on the decorative chain around his neck. President Timmons had given both the Pip and the necklace to him, as a gift to mark the occasion of his union with her "baby sister." The way Mac felt right now, he'd have liked to rip the chain from his neck and toss it into the Pacific Ocean, but he resisted the urge. The Pip was his lifeline, his best source for information about this primitive world, and his only hope of transporting back to the world he'd left behind.

He activated his Pip, ordering it to stop sending out the audio waves that were keeping Ariel unconscious. Pip deactivated the sleep-induction program, and Mac watched as Ariel slowly awoke. She rubbed her eyes, and wriggled a little on the hard ground before sitting up. The black garment she was wearing twisted upward, exposing several centimeters of her slender thighs, and the slight curve of her buttocks. He looked away, surprised that he'd experienced a brief, inexplicable surge of sexual desire. How odd, he thought, that covering the body with pieces of woven cloth should actually create feelings of erotic arousal.

Ariel was still only semiconscious when he helped her to her feet. She looked at him blearily, but her gaze focused almost at once, and he could see that she was reacting to his presence with an emotion somewhere between acute fear and secret laughter. He wasn't sure which emotion annoyed him more.

"Something amuses you?" he asked stiffly, knowing that he sounded like a pompous jackass when he was forced to speak English, a language that hadn't been in common use for a decade before his birth. "I would be honored if you would share the joke."

"Er . . . no joke. It's nothing, really. Nothing at all." Her voice was husky with suppressed laughter even as she uttered the lies.

Mac felt a surge of frustration. It bothered him that Ariel should find him an object of ridicule. It bothered him even more that she was too afraid of him to admit it.

"I wish you would accept that I am neither a fool nor a lunatic," he said quietly. "Merely a man who finds himself struggling to understand the customs of another time and another place. What have I done to amuse you?" His mouth twisted in wry self-mockery. "I promise that I will not zap you with my ray gun if I don't like your answer."

A faint trace of pink colored her cheeks. "You don't have a ray gun."

He glanced at the laser 2-gig magnum tucked into the waistband of his pants. If only she knew. "Yes, I do. But the power coil doesn't seem to work here in your world, if that makes you feel any safer. Now, tell me why you were laughing at me."

Her eyes narrowed impatiently as she glanced at his laser-gig, but her mouth still quirked with hidden laughter. "If you really don't know, Mac, you're wearing women's clothes."

Astonished, he inspected the lacy ruffles on his shirt. "Women's clothes? How can you tell?"

She rolled her eyes. "It's kind of easy, Mac. The daisies on your yellow pants are the first clue, and the frills on your pink blouse don't exactly send a subtle message. Combine that with the silver body paint, and your appearance is . . . eye-catching . . . to say the least."

He could accept that his silver skin looked out of place, but he could see nothing at all wrong with his clothes. Mac tugged irritably at the seam of his pants. "These are trousers, a male garment," he said. "In Europe and the Americas, women wore skirts and men wore pants until almost the middle of the twenty-first century. I remember seeing dozens of pictures in my history books. It is only in Asia that the pattern was sometimes reversed. In Asia, men of high social rank often wore skirts and peasant women wore pants."

She shook her head. "I don't know anything about the twenty-first century, Mac, and I'm sure you don't, either. But this is America, not Asia, and we're in 1996. Trust me, men don't wear flowered pants, and they don't wear pink ruffles. Flowers and frills signal that the person wearing them is a woman."

His puzzlement deepened. "Are you suggesting that without flowers and ruffles to designate a female wearer, the citizens of your time could not distinguish between a man and a woman? There are surely many visible differences that fabric does not conceal. For example, a man does not have enlarged breasts, suitable for the suckling of infants and a woman does not have a pen—"

"For heaven's sake! Of course we can tell the difference between men and woman whatever they're wearing!" She gave a husky little laugh. "Never mind, Mac. If the concept is too difficult for you, don't try to grasp it. Just accept that men don't wear yellow rayon pants, dotted with daisies, okay?"

"That is a pity, since flowers make a most attractive design, and one which we often incorporate into our permapel. But I thank you for the lesson, Ariel." He swept her up into his arms, impatient with a distinction that seemed trivial to him.

"It is time for us to return to your home, and there is no time for me to change," he said. "Besides, I have no idea of where

I would find the necessary male garments. All that matters is that I no longer stand out from the crowd because of my naked genitals."

"Sure, Mac. You're real inconspicuous." Ariel gave him one of those glances that indicated she was quite sure he was crazy. He ignored the look. It was simply a variation on the same one she'd been giving him all morning and Mac was becoming rather tired of it.

He activated his Pip, feeling an immature burst of pleasure when he visualized Ariel's reaction to the technological marvels he could summon, even cut off from most of the benefits of his civilization. Now that he'd learned what time frame he was operating in, accurate information was relatively easy to access. Unfortunately, he was not sure how complete the information was. His Pip, although it had been programmed with basic survival skills, was more of an entertainment device for a couple celebrating their Silver Ceremony.

"Search for highway-system route maps, southern California, year 1996," he said. "Project map in visual mode, indicating location of a Marine Corps base known as Camp Pendleton, and my point of entry into the Pacific Ocean at 21:35 last night. Also indicate nearest transportation center."

Pip obligingly projected a map onto the patch of flat, sandy ground where Ariel had been sleeping. A red pulsating circle indicated their current location. A red asterisk marked the shoreline some twenty-four kilometers to the north, and a note explained that this was the point at which Mac and an accompanying, unidentified female had entered the ocean. The nearest town to the asterisk seemed to be a place called San Clemente.

"No public transportation centers located in this region," Pip announced in a brisk, expressionless tone. "Two hundred vehicles capable of providing automated transportation are located 4.45 kilometers to the northeast."

Mac couldn't help enjoying Ariel's reaction to his little demonstration of twenty-second-century technology. Her amusement had vanished in a trice the moment the map appeared on the ground. Disbelief, fear and curiosity chased each other across her expressive features.

"Wh-what is that?" she asked, pointing from his Pip to the map. "How did you . . . make that appear?"

"I asked Pip to show us a map of southern California in the year 1996. I wanted to know the location of the nearest highway and public-transportation center so that I could determine the quickest way to take you home."

She stared at the map, her face pale. "What is a—pip?" Her voice sounded gruff. He could tell she was having a hard time keeping it steady.

"Pip is an acronym for Personal Information Provider," he said, holding out the glowing silver tube so that she could see it more clearly. "In my world, every citizen carries at least one Pip at all times."

"So that the government can keep track of you?" she asked.

He shook his head. "The opposite. So that we can keep track of the world around us. We can buy different types of Pip, programmed to provide different types of information."

She reached out to touch the Pip, then snatched back her hand as she felt the subtle pulse of its power cell. "What's that decoration engraved on the side of . . . it?" she asked.

"That is the official seal of the president of the United Republic of the Americas. President Timmons gave me this Pip as a Silver Ceremony gift." He felt bleakness sweep over him. "It is programmed with a variety of entertainment features, and a great deal of helpful information for new parents."

She looked away, her expression somewhere between weary and exasperated and he realized she'd stopped believing him again. He gave the order for Pip to deactivate. A light pulsed for a fraction of a second at the end of the Pip, and the map disappeared.

Mac tucked the device under the ruffled neckline of his shirt. "I think in your time my Pip would be referred to as a portable micro-minicomputer," he said. "Perhaps, if you think of it in that way, it will not seem so extraordinary, but merely a development of a tool already known to you. Rather like your planes that fly across continents were developed from the first primitive engines that powered railway engines for hauling coal."

She glanced at his Pip once more. Then she blinked, and stared straight ahead, her jaw rigid. "It took two hundred years to go from steam engines to planes," she said.

"And it took two hundred years to go from the first vacuum-tube computer to the early model of the Pip," Mac told her.

"It's only been fifty years since the first computer was built in a laboratory."

"For you it's only been fifty years. For me it has been more than two centuries."

Ariel didn't respond and Mac felt absurdly pleased that, for once, she hadn't given him a look that informed him he was crazy. His masculine ego perked up a bit after twenty-four hours of relentless mauling. Feeling almost cheerful, he swung her into his arms and stepped out at a brisk pace in the direction of the vehicle-storage area Pip had indicated. Ariel remained so still in his arms that he looked down at her, half expecting to discover that she'd succumbed to yet another unsuspected weakness of her frail twentieth-century physique.

Fortunately, she gave no sign of being ill, just seemed to be deep in thought. She returned his gaze, her hazel eyes huge in her face, her soft full lips quivering slightly. He'd been so overwhelmed by events since he arrived in her time that he'd barely considered Ariel as a woman, and he realized with a shock that, when she recovered from her injuries, she would be exceptionally beautiful.

"Why are you looking at me like that?" she asked, her voice low.

"I wished to be sure that you were feeling in good health despite your silence."

"I'm fine, except for my sprained ankle."

"That is good. I am sorry that you must suffer pain, but I have no medical supplies with me, and this Pip carries only the most basic first-aid program."

"I have an elastic bandage at home, which should help some. Although I probably should get an X-ray to see if I've broken anything."

"There is no need for an X-ray. Pip scanned the injury and you have no broken bones."

She didn't say anything, but the blood rushed into her cheeks, turning them darkly pink. He found the sight enchanting. He wondered how she would react if he told her that in his century, only the most intimate of partners ever saw their lovers without a layer of permapel covering their faces, and that the bare skin of her face struck him as blatantly erotic.

He looked quickly away, disciplining his thoughts. Consuela Timmons would soon have the twentieth-century cops running full cry on his tail, and he had no time to indulge in sexual fantasies.

Ariel broke the short silence. "Mac, what language were you speaking just now?" she asked.

He smiled wryly. "I hoped that it was English," he said.

"No, I didn't mean the language you spoke to me. What language did you use when you gave instructions to your...minicomputer. It didn't sound as if you were speaking English at all."

"That's because I wasn't," he said. "In my century, we speak Spanglish throughout all the regions that make up the United Republic of the Americas."

"Spanglish?" she repeated doubtfully. "A mixture of Spanish and English, do you mean?"

"Spanish and English are the dominating influences in our language, but there's a generous pinch of Portuguese, inherited from our Brazilian citizens, and a dash of French from Quebec. Not to mention all the Asian words that came into the language from Korean and Chinese immigrants during the early twenty-first century."

"You mean it's an invented language, with bits and pieces taken from all the languages people in America speak?"

"I'm not sure 'invented' is the correct way to describe how Spanglish came into existence. By the time the countries of our hemisphere officially united to form the Republic of the Americas, the various peoples had migrated and intermarried to such an extent that most of us were already speaking a universal patois just so that we could understand each other. The patois was despised by some self-appointed language purists and by nearly all government officials. The purists protested for as long as they could, but eventually Spanglish became accepted as the official language of our country. Right after the Great Famine, in fact, when few people had the energy to insist on linguistic purity, or anything else except finding sufficient sources of food."

"But you speak English, Mac."

"Every citizen in every country in the world is required to study English for a minimum of eight years," Mac said. "It has been decreed the world's common language by the United

Nations. Students cannot graduate from university without demonstrating fluency in English, whatever their course of study, or whatever the language of their birth happens to be. But although my job requires me to read many documents written in English, I rarely have occasion to speak it, and the words do not come easily to my tongue."

"You make your society sound so real," Ariel said, and there was a note akin to despair in her voice. "You truly believe you're a time traveler from the end of the twenty-second century, don't you, Mac?"

"I make my society sound real because it is real," he replied. "I believe that I have traveled back through time because that is the truth."

"But time travel is impossible," she said.

"For your time, but not for mine." He touched her lightly on the forehead, wanting to smooth away the worried creases, wishing he could somehow compel her to trust him. "You can accept that I am a time traveler, Ariel, or you can decide that I am crazy. It will not change the truth, of course, but it will undoubtedly change how you respond to me. You must ask yourself a simple question. Do you truly believe I am a madman?"

"I don't know what I believe." She drew in a shallow breath. "You want me to trust you, Mac, but you've never offered me a choice about staying with you. I'd be a foolish prisoner if I started to trust everything my jailer tells me."

"It is, perhaps, equally foolish to assume that everything your jailer says must be a lie."

"At least you don't deny that you're holding me prisoner."

Mac looked down at her. "I have taken you into protective custody, Ariel. I believe that even in the twentieth century protective custody is a legal concept everyone understands."

"Protective custody?" she said angrily. "For heaven's sake, Mac, I was there, remember? Do you expect me to believe that when you took me hostage and jumped into the Pacific Ocean, you did it to protect me?"

"But of course I did," he said. "What other possible motive could I have for risking my safety by taking you with me?"

"Oh, give me a break," she said. "You used my body as a shield, Mac. You used me as a hostage to ward off the people who were trying to capture you."

"A hostage! What nonsense is this? You have completely misunderstood my actions!" he exclaimed.

"But you warned people to keep away!"

"From you, not from me! None of those people could have taken me captive. It is laughable that you should suggest it. Once Consuela was unconscious, I was never at risk. I am trained to repel physical attack, permapel resists penetration, and with one touch of my knife, I could have sliced to the bone the flesh of anyone who threatened me. It was you whom I sought to protect. I took you with me strictly for your own safety."

"Who are you protecting me from?" she asked sarcastically. "Space aliens? Hordes of marauding time travelers?"

"From just one time traveler," he said quietly. "Namely, Consuela Timmons. Who will undoubtedly try to kill you as soon as she is released from the hospital."

"Consuela Timmons isn't going to be released from the hospital," Ariel said tiredly. "I've told you, Mac, she can't possibly survive the wounds she sustained. She's no threat to either of us because I'm sure she's dead."

"And I am equally sure that she is not." Mac would have argued with her some more, but he saw a large building on the other side of the street, surrounded by a huge open space, filled with empty vehicles. Obviously the vehicle-storage area. Wonderful! Now they would be able to drive to Ariel's housing unit, instead of walking for another twenty kilometers. Mac would have liked to explain why Consuela was most unlikely to be dead, to explain the healing powers of genetically enhanced human bodies in the twenty-second century, and the medical options available to Consuela, but he decided this was not the time. Later, when they were safely hidden behind the protective walls of Ariel's housing unit, he would try to make her understand. He crossed the road and walked up to the nearest automobile, which was painted white, like many of the other vehicles in the transportation center.

"What does the color white signify?" he asked Ariel.

She looked at him blankly. "I don't understand your question, Mac."

"This automobile is painted white. Does the color white indicate that the vehicle will travel a certain designated distance?" he asked. "Or is there some other significance to the color?"

"It doesn't signify anything, except that its owner likes white."

"Then this vehicle is already serviced and ready to travel the twenty kilometers to your housing unit?" he asked.

She was back to looking at him as if he was crazy. "Mac, you aren't planning to steal this car, are you?"

"Of course not." Where in the world did she come up with such strange ideas about his ethics? "I will return the vehicle to the nearest transportation center as soon as we reach our destination."

"What transportation center are you talking about?"

Conversations with Ariel really were difficult to follow. "Whatever one is closest to your housing unit," he explained with as much patience as he could muster. He tugged at the handle of the car. Nothing happened. He shrugged and told Pip to unlock the door. A primitive locking device inserted into the side panel unlatched at once. He bent down, and pushed Ariel across the seat into the passenger side of the vehicle.

"If you're not stealing this car, would you mind telling me what you are doing?" Ariel demanded.

"Trying to get you home," he said, getting more and more impatient at the need to explain the obvious. This was her century, not his. Didn't she recognize a transportation center when she saw one? Didn't she drive in these terrifying automobiles on a daily basis? He was getting mighty tired of struggling to make himself understood, and even more tired of the constant fear that Consuela was planning major mischief while he stood around, trying unsuccessfully to convince Ariel that he wasn't crazy.

Mac decided to quit with the explanations, which Ariel never believed, anyway. He followed her into the car, slamming the doors shut. At his command, Pip reclosed the locks. He ordered Pip to take the vehicle out of the transportation center. Pip glowed and beeped, then relapsed into uncommunicative silence.

Oh great, now what? Didn't Pip know how to drive the car? Mac viewed the instrument panel with alarm. He would never have admitted it to Ariel, but the controls of the vehicle looked terrifyingly complex. He knew that the old-fashioned fossil-fuel engine needed to be turned on manually, but he couldn't see anything that might be an ignition switch.

"Pip, find the vehicle ignition," he ordered.

Pip burped again, then retreated into obstinate silence. The car obviously didn't have sufficient electronic parts for Pip to make it function. Ariel, meanwhile, was pounding on the window, yelling at the top of her lungs in an effort to attract the attention of a middle-aged couple just now emerging from the two-story brick structure in the center of the vehicle-storage area.

Unfortunately, she seemed to be succeeding. The couple hurried toward the car, their facial expressions and body language both displaying alarm.

There was an antiquated keyhole on the steel shaft that attached the steering wheel to the engine. Could this be the ignition-control switch? Mac decided he'd fooled around long enough. He informed Pip that this was the ignition lock and gave him five seconds to turn it on.

Pip seemed to like this instruction better than the earlier ones. Within three seconds, the gasoline fired and the vehicle engine hummed to life.

Great. Mac had an activated automobile now, but he hadn't the faintest idea how to guide the damn thing out of its docking station. The middle-aged couple were close enough to have gotten a good look at him, and he could see their alarmed expressions change rapidly to total horror. He wasted a precious moment thinking that the absence of permapel made emotions almost embarrassingly visible on people's faces.

The man stepped up to the car, pulling on the door handle, and the woman ran back to the building she'd left only moments earlier. Trouble was definitely brewing.

Mac gave the vehicle every start-up command he could think of. Nothing happened. The engine continued to hum, but the car didn't move. When he thought of all that was at stake if he didn't get out of here, Mac felt himself start to sweat hard enough that the permapel had a tough time equalizing his body temperature. Ariel, oddly, had subsided into a tense and wary silence. Suddenly, she turned and grabbed a lever sticking out from behind the steering wheel.

"You have to put the engine in gear before it will move," she said tightly. "Okay, I've put it into reverse. Now press your right foot on the accelerator and back out. Slowly. No! My God, Mac! Watch out for the other cars!"

There was a hideous sound of tearing metal as the car skewed sideways and slammed into the vehicle docked in the next station. Good grief, the other vehicles didn't even have a control program to prevent docking-station collisions! Mac was still trying to decide which mystifying button or lever he should press to extricate themselves without inflicting further damage on the neighboring automobile, when Ariel grabbed his arm and shoved him toward the rear seat.

"Get into the back and stay there," she said. "I'll drive us home. If this damn car's still drivable, that is."

The woman had reappeared on the steps of the central structure and her partner's shouts had attracted a small crowd of angry observers. Mac made a swift mental review of his options and decided he had no choice than to hope Ariel meant to cooperate with him. He climbed into the rear of the car, and watched as Ariel slid across into the driver's seat.

"Thank goodness it's my left ankle that's sprained," she muttered. "Uh-oh, look! There's a guy with a cellular phone. He's probably calling the cops right now."

Mac wished he could remember what a cellular phone was. It didn't sound good. With what he considered spectacular hand-eye coordination, not to mention mechanical skill, Ariel extricated their car from its entanglement with its neighbor, and backed out into an open space, where she maneuvered the gear levers and swung the car around so that it was moving forward. In less than twenty seconds, they had squeezed into the flow of vehicles traveling on the narrow highway, tooling forward at a speed of almost eighty kilometers an hour.

He could see that Ariel was watching him in the little mirror suspended to the side of her. Mac tried not to panic. "Should you not direct your attention to the roadway ahead of you?" he asked. He swallowed hard. "The potential for a serious accident in this vehicle is very high."

Ariel actually grinned. "You're scared, aren't you?"

"Scared? No, of course I am not scared. You are simply driving several hundredweight of uncontrolled metal parts down a gravel highway, but no doubt that is no reason for me to feel concern for our safety."

Ariel leaned back in the driver's seat, but at least she looked straight ahead of her for several comforting moments. Then she turned her gaze back to the mirror. Mac tried not to appear humiliatingly terrified. It seemed that he failed.

"Okay," she said. "You win, Mac. Nobody could fake that much terror. You've never been in a car before, have you?"

"Only in a museum," he admitted. "And not when it was in motion."

She shook her head as if trying to clear her fuzzy thoughts. "You really have traveled back in time, haven't you?"

"Yes."

"My God, I'm having a conversation with someone who won't exist for another two hundred years or so."

"Time is not linear except in our perception of it," Mac told her. He cleared his throat. "Ariel, I'm delighted that you now believe I am indeed a traveler from the twenty-second century, but have you noticed that there is a large truck approaching us at a very high speed?"

She laughed. "I've noticed. Don't worry about it, Mac. It's on the other side of the road."

She was actually enjoying this. She wasn't even marginally frightened. The truck belched a cloud of black smoke. Ariel paid no heed. She punched a button on the control panel and the sound of an ancient song filled the automobile. Ariel started to hum the melody.

Mac closed his eyes. She was actually having fun. One thing, it seemed, could be counted on whether you found yourself in 1996, or 2196. The ways of women were totally incomprehensible to the inferior male mind.

4

"THIS IS where I live," Ariel said, turning the car into the small complex that contained her town house. By some benevolent whim of fate, her neighborhood in Laguna Hills had survived the ravages of California's floods, brushfires and earthquakes unscathed. With the azaleas in the central courtyard beginning to bloom, and the sun glinting invitingly off the clear blue waters of the swimming pool, she could almost remember why L.A. had once seemed such a great place to live.

She parked the stolen Toyota Celica in a space marked Visitors, half expecting to hear the wail of a police siren, or to see a cop spring out from behind the pool cabana to arrest her for aiding and abetting a murderer. Lord knew, Mac's silver skin made him easy to identify. The couple they'd encountered in the Camp Pendleton parking lot would have no difficulty in describing him, and by now, the police would be hot on his tail. Unfortunately, they weren't likely to show her much sympathy when they finally caught up with her. The moment she sat behind the wheel of the stolen Toyota and drove away, she had become Mac's accomplice instead of his victim.

Even though she'd just spent almost an hour driving home with Mac, she still couldn't quite grasp the fact that she'd actively helped him to escape. How had such a thing happened? Of all the women in Los Angeles, Ariel Hutton had to head the list of least likely allies for a fugitive who claimed to be a time traveler from the twenty-second century.

Time traveler. Good grief! Her stomach lurched every time she thought those ridiculous words. Ariel smiled grimly as she unlatched her seat belt. The cops would have to hurry if they wanted to arrest her before the men in white coats carted her away.

She reached for the key to turn off the ignition, then remembered there was no key. "Could Pip turn off the ignition, please," she asked Mac, her voice taut. There, she'd done it. She'd acknowledged that the glowing medallion hanging around Mac's neck actually had the power to do things like turn car engines on and off by remote control.

Mac murmured a command and the engine cut off. She wasn't sure if it made her feel better or worse to know that Pip had done precisely what she'd asked. The moment the engine died, Mac got out of the car. He spoke quickly, his voice tense. "If you tell me which one of these housing units is yours, I will carry you there. We must hurry, before we are observed."

His nervousness reminded Ariel yet again that Mac was a wanted fugitive, that last night he had slashed open a woman's throat and jumped into the sea to avoid capture. And yet, this morning, she was ready to invite this same violent man into her home. She wondered at what point in time she had crossed over from being mildly loony to totally nuts. She looked up at Mac, resolved to get a grip on her common sense and send him away.

"My town house is the second door on the left, number 103," she heard herself say, and realized she had just thrown away her last chance to escape from a dangerous lunatic.

He bent down to pick her up, but she shook her head. "There's no need for you to carry me, Mac. I can walk, if you'll give me a little bit of help."

He surprised her by agreeing without any argument. "Very well," he said, extending his arm. "I'll walk slowly and you can hop. But let us not hang around, if you please."

The muscles of his arm flowed and rippled beneath the layer of permapel as he extended his arm. It was oddly attractive to feel every tiny movement of his body without any accompanying sensation of skin, or bodily heat. Interesting stuff, permapel, once you got used to it. In fact, Mac's silver skin no longer looked all that strange to her, Ariel realized, and she was developing quite a fondness for his flowered pants and pink ruffled blouse. He wore them with a certain indefinable panache.

Irritated by the eccentricity of her thoughts, she hopped in determined silence toward her town house. When they were at her door, Mac turned her around to face him. He looked down at her for a brief, silent moment. Then he touched her very lightly on the cheek.

"I thank you for your kindness in taking me into your home, Ariel."

"You're welcome." She looked away, because her knees suddenly felt as shaky as her sprained ankle.

Mac's voice deepened. "Before we enter your home, I wish you to know that your kindness will be honored. You have my promise that I will give my life to keep you safe from the harm that Consuela threatens."

"Er...thank you, Mac, I appreciate the thought." Ariel offered a brief prayer of thanks that Consuela was almost certainly dead and therefore unlikely to test Mac's skills as a protector, much less require him to make any ultimate sacrifices. Given that the guy had flinched every time she overtook a car during the drive home, had covered his head with his hands when she passed a garbage truck and had trembled whenever she took the Toyota to any speed over fifty, he might not be the most effective bodyguard in the world.

Still, he couldn't help his phobias, and he seemed to have made the offer in all sincerity. She smiled at him.

"I guess we have a small problem with getting into my house, though, Mac. I don't have a front-door key. And—oh, Lord!—there's Brenda Lewinski, my next-door neighbor. She has to be the biggest snoop west of the Mississippi. Damn! She's heading straight for us."

Mac muttered something incomprehensible and his gaze narrowed for an instant, but he made no effort to avoid Brenda, who was staring at the pair of them with her mouth hanging wide open.

"Good morning to you," Mac said with amazing aplomb, given the circumstances. Since he was still supporting Ariel, it couldn't exactly be said that he swept Brenda a bow, but he came darn close.

"G-good morning." Brenda's mouth closed, but her eyes threatened to pop out of their sockets. "My God, Ariel, what happened? Every TV station in the city announced that you were drowned! They said on the 'Today' show that some guy dressed in a silver space suit kidnapped you from your sister's hous—"

She broke off abruptly, and stared at Mac in dawning horror. "It's you!" she gasped. "You're the space alien who made off with Ariel! But they said you'd both drowned!" Brenda looked as if she would succumb to screaming hysterics if only she could find the breath.

"The news announcements were in error," Mac said coolly. "There is no cause for alarm, I assure you. As you can see, we are very much alive. And I am certainly not a space alien. In fact, I have never left planet Earth, except for one brief and extremely boring trip to the moon."

"The m-moon? You think you've been to the moon?" Brenda didn't wait to argue. She turned to flee just as Mac gave his Pip a murmured command. As far as Ariel could see,

Pip didn't respond, but Brenda stopped running and collapsed against the stucco wall of her town house, sliding slowly toward the ground until she was lying in a limp heap on the flagstoned walkway.

"Oh, God, what have you done to her?" Ariel asked, hopping toward her unconscious neighbor. "Have you k-killed her?"

"Of course not!" Mac sounded outraged. "I have sent her to sleep, that's all. You see, she is breathing normally. Pip is emitting a sound wave aimed directly at Brenda, and pitched at a frequency that induces sleep and pleasant dreams. I used the same technique on you, at the beach. When we leave here, I will deactivate the signal and she will wake up, refreshed and totally unharmed. Just as you did."

"Will she remember seeing us?"

"Unfortunately, yes, unless she manages to convince herself that she was dreaming." Mac scooped Brenda up, and slung her over his shoulder. Brenda was tall and plump, but he seemed to find her no more troublesome to carry than he'd found Ariel. He gave a quick command to his Pip and a beam of intense white light pierced the lock on Ariel's front door. She heard the tumblers fall into alignment and the door swung open as soon as she turned the handle.

"Can't you put Brenda in her own house?" she asked as Mac pushed the door shut with his foot, and carried Brenda across the tiled entryway and into Ariel's small living room.

He shook his head. "This type of Pip can't keep the sound wave sufficiently focused except over short distances," he said. "Unfortunately, my Pip is designed for recreation, not law enforcement. When chasing after Consuela, I had no time to stop and pick up equipment."

He deposited Brenda on the sofa and folded her hands neatly in her lap. "There, she'll be quite comfortable. Now, where is your shower room? You need to wash all the sea salt

off your skin, and then I will restrap your ankle with...
whatever substance you use for such purposes."

A hot shower sounded beyond wonderful, and Ariel
pointed out the stairs that led to her bedroom and attached
bathroom. Mac carried her upstairs at his usual run. "I can
manage now, thanks," she said when he deposited her on the
only available seat in the bathroom, which happened to be
the toilet.

"Of course you can't manage alone," he said, using the
point of his knife to rip through the makeshift brace on her
ankle. He set the scraps of dress and driftwood in the sink,
then began stripping off his blouse and flowered pants without the slightest hint that he'd remembered her lectures about
men and women not appearing naked in front of each other.

"Please undress yourself, Ariel," he said, draping his blouse
over the edge of the bath. "I will carry you into the shower
with me and make sure that you do not fall."

She stared at him, torn between annoyance and a perverse
thrill of physical awareness. She should have gotten used to
seeing him naked by now, but apparently she hadn't. His
masculinity seemed overwhelming in the confines of her
bathroom, and, given that he'd been carrying her around for
the best part of the morning, she couldn't quite understand
the reason for her sudden urge to discover what it would feel
like to press up against his body when it was wet and slick
with soap and hot water.

She looked down at her hands, and gulped in a shaky
breath, struggling for control. She was thirty-three years old,
a pillar of the community. She didn't—she absolutely
didn't—need to take a shower with a silver-coated time traveler.

"Er...Mac...I can manage on my own, thanks. You can
use the shower when I've finished. There's a little guest bathroom downstairs if you need to wash up, or anything. Why

don't you have a drink, or something to eat? You'll find fruit juice and stuff in the fridge. I'll call you when I'm done. Close the bathroom door on your way out."

"We have already agreed that you can't manage on your own," he said, sounding both puzzled and annoyed. "How will you get into the shower? Look, there's a sill you must step over. You might slip on the wet tile and fall. In view of your injured ankle, I must hold you while you wash yourself, that is obvious."

Ariel blushed at the images his suggestion evoked. "Mac, listen to me. Let's go through this one more time, slowly, from the top. In my world, men don't help women to take a shower when the two of them have only just met. It's not the way things work in the 1990s, okay?"

He shook his head. "The ways of your world are most foolish. I cannot allow you to injure yourself again, so we shall follow the customs of my time instead of yours. Besides, I'm still wearing my permapel, so I won't be naked. You have no reason for concern."

Ariel counted silently to ten. "But I'm not wearing permapel, Mac. And a layer of fancy goo doesn't constitute clothing, not in my world. So, as far as I'm concerned, you're buck naked!"

"Your perceptions are distorted," he said. "Permapel is a far more efficient barrier than cloth. It permits the wearer only a limited sense of touch, except in the hands, where it is necessary for safety reasons to retain full sensation. Under the circumstances, sexual intimacy is almost impossible as long as a person is wearing permapel."

"That's debatable. And I still don't want you in the shower with me."

"But fear of sexual intimacy is why your society is so afraid of naked bodies, is it not? You are afraid that if I see your reproductive organs, I'll wish to mate with you." He gave her a friendly smile. "Do not be alarmed, Ariel. I can assure you, I will have no such sexual urges. You forget, our society has different standards from yours and I have already seen your naked face, so your body is certainly not going to propel me into a state of uncontrolled lust."

Because he found her face so unattractive that he couldn't imagine becoming aroused by the rest of her? Mac's latest attempt at reassurance left Ariel speechless, which was probably fortunate, given what she might otherwise have said. He picked her up, ignoring her squeaks of protest, and carried her into the shower stall, closing the glass door behind them. She pummeled his chest in a gesture that was becoming as familiar as it was futile.

"You will hurt your fingers," he said calmly. "Don't do that, Ariel." He set her down so that she was leaning against the tiled wall and reached behind her to unzip the ragged remains of her black evening dress. His torso pressed full length against hers. Ariel discovered a sudden difficulty in breathing, which wasn't improved when Mac gave a throaty, satisfied little chuckle.

It turned out, though, that his chuckles weren't precipitated by a rush of sexual desire, but by the intricacies of her zipper. He swiveled her around so that he could see her back, then slid the zipper up and down a couple of times, smiling delightedly.

"Your clothing is made with ingenious devices for closure," he said, pulling her dress over her head. He tossed it over the shower door and reached for the hook on her bra, once again totally ignoring her objections. Perhaps because they were so feeble.

He mastered the front hook on her bra and smiled, like a child with a new toy. "They are most amusing, these gadgets that hold cloth together."

It was bizarre to think of her zipper and favorite bra as entertaining museum curiosities. Ariel supposed that must be why she forgot to protest what Mac was doing. She couldn't think of any other good reason for her to stand right next to him and fail to scream, yell or otherwise complain while he took off her clothes. He was pushing aside the lacy cups of her bra and starting to slide the straps off her shoulders, when she finally gathered her scattered wits and wriggled away from him. She caught him unawares, and as he steadied himself, his hands brushed over her naked breasts, the tips of his fingers grazing her nipples. Her whole body tensed in instant reaction.

For a single fraught moment, they stared at each other, eyes wide, his hands still cupping her breasts, neither of them seemingly able to move. Then he stepped back, his hands falling to his sides, but his gaze remaining locked with hers. He drew in a deep, slow breath, as if getting ready to speak, but for once, he seemed at a loss for words.

Ariel closed her eyes, unable to subdue the chaotic whirl of her emotions or the sudden fire that burned in her veins. Get a life, she ordered herself. He hardly touched you. He sure as heck wasn't coming on to you, and you know it.

The silence had gone on far too long. In the end, it seemed easiest to be angry. "Get out of the shower," she said through clenched teeth. "I haven't consented to your being in here with me, Mac, and I don't want you to undress me. In *my* time, in *my* world, what you're doing is illegal—"

"You need say nothing more." He pushed open the glass door and stepped out of the shower, his expression unreadable behind his mask of permapel. "I'm sorry," he said quietly. "You're right to be angry, Ariel. I should not ignore your customs simply because they make no sense to me. The only excuse for my behavior is that I have caused you much harm and I'm worried lest you slip and fall."

"I won't fall."

He placed his hand on his heart and inclined his head in the gesture that was beginning to seem a natural part of him. "Then I will go downstairs and wait for you in the living room." He gave a faint smile. "Your friend Brenda and I can snooze together."

The bathroom door closed softly. Ariel slumped against the wall of the shower, turning the water on full power and squirting shampoo into her hair with manic energy. After ten minutes of being pounded by hot water, she felt like a semi-normal human being, with an almost functional brain.

She absolutely, positively, was not attracted to Mac, she told herself. Good grief, she was years past the stage of getting turned on by rippling muscles and demonstrations of brute strength. Besides, the guy had silver skin, talked funny, was scared of driving in a car, zapped people with his necklace—and she didn't even want to contemplate what he might consider a normal sexual relationship.

She gave herself a final brisk rub with the towel and disciplined herself to concentrate on more important matters than Mac's impressive pecs and surprisingly gentle fingers. Scowling, she yanked open the bathroom cabinet. Fortunately, she'd managed to avoid the ravages of sunburn, and once she'd slathered moisturizing cream all over her face and body, her skin felt only a little bit worse for wear. Her thick, light brown hair spiked around her head like a cartoon drawing of somebody who'd stuck her finger into an electrical socket, but she sprayed on instant conditioner until she finally managed to drag a comb through it and unsnarl all the tangles.

When she'd finished blowing it dry, her hair seemed unusually fluffy, blurring the angles of her face and making it appear softer. Perhaps it was all the fresh air that left her cheeks flushed and her hazel eyes sparking with an intriguing flash of green. She touched her lips with the tips of her fingers, then shook her head, disconcerted by this unaccustomed fascination with her own appearance.

Ariel pulled a mocking face at the mirror. She'd long ago resigned herself to the fact that fate had arranged her features in a pallid imitation of Miranda's lush brunette beauty. Clever eye makeup and a less severe hairstyle wasn't suddenly going to transform her into a raving sex symbol. Which, of course, was the last thing she wanted to be transformed into, anyway. Ariel had tried sex several times, and found it vastly overrated.

"Enough of this," she muttered. She closed the door of the bathroom cabinet with enough force to rattle the glass. Finding a roll of adhesive elastic bandage amongst her first-aid supplies, she strapped her ankle firmly enough to stop the ache, although it still felt too weak to walk on.

Bundled into a toweling robe, she stuck her head around the door and called downstairs to Mac. Carefully avoiding even a glance in his direction, she informed him that she was finished in the bathroom if he wanted to take his shower. Having delivered her message, she escaped through the other door into her bedroom.

This was her favorite room in her small town house, the room that almost made her giant mortgage payment bearable. She loved the alcove that she'd furnished as an office space, with an antique desk salvaged from a garage sale. She loved the French doors that opened onto a balcony filled with flowers in tubs, as well as the luxurious velvet-sheared carpet, the clean white walls and the brightly embroidered throw pillows tossed on the puffy comforter of her king-size bed.

Miranda had raised an inquiring eyebrow when she saw the giant bed, but Ariel hadn't answered her sister's unspoken question. The truth was, Ariel might consider sex overrated, but she believed in being prepared for all possibilities.

She wanted to be sure that if she ever found a man she was willing to invite into her bed, they wouldn't keep bumping into each other during the night. Having grown up in assorted communes, not to mention the memorable summer when her parents had decided to get closer to nature by living in a tent, Ariel valued her privacy. Touching during sex was okay, but she certainly didn't want to keep encountering male body parts while she was sleeping.

So far, in the two years since she'd moved into her town house, her preparations for comfortable sleeping arrangements had been unnecessary. Ariel was beginning to suspect she was holding out for the unattainable. She didn't expect Kevin Costner or Brad Pitt, but she did want a responsible man with a solid career, no hang-ups about his last wife, willing to become the father of at least two children. Unfortunately, such men didn't seem to be among the crops California grew with any degree of success.

She rummaged through her closet searching for a nifty yellow linen skirt with a coordinating cotton-knit sweater she'd bought only a week ago. When she realized that she was looking for a brand-new outfit simply to impress Mac, she gave up hunting for the yellow skirt and sweater, and put on a pair of shorts and a shirt that had seen better days. She'd be damned if she was going to strut around in special clothes for a guy who considered silver glop the ultimate dress-for-success outfit.

Which reminded her that Mac was going to need a set of men's clothes once he got out of the shower. She rummaged around in her closet once more, and found a pair of sneakers and a pair of sweatpants left behind from her father's last visit, and going through her drawers, she found an oversize T-shirt that she hoped might be large enough to accommodate Mac's shoulders. Unfortunately, male underwear was beyond her resources. Bundling the clothes under her arm, she stuck them around the bathroom door in a place where Mac couldn't avoid seeing them.

She closed the door before he noticed her, and hopped downstairs, clinging to the banisters, relieved that her bandaged ankle was finally able to take some of her weight.

Having assured herself that Brenda was still safely sleeping, she headed for the kitchen and poured herself a large glass of orange juice. Boy, did it ever taste heavenly! She hadn't realized how dehydrated her body was until she actually started drinking. Her stomach rumbled with sudden hunger, and she was taking a luxurious bite out of a large apple, when she caught sight of the phone hanging on the kitchen wall, and remembered that Miranda and Ralph had no idea she was alive.

Horrified that she'd delayed even this long in letting them know she was safe, she quickly dialed their unlisted personal number. Frustratingly, she got the hum of a busy signal. Still munching on her apple, she dialed again.

"What are you doing?"

Startled because she hadn't heard Mac's approach, her head jerked up. Juggling the phone and the apple, she managed to drop them both, her gaze widening as he came into the kitchen. "Oh, my," she said, putting down her half-eaten apple. "Oh, my!"

"Is something the matter?" Mac asked, returning the phone to the hook.

"You . . . took off your layer of permapel," she said. She forced the words out, although her lungs felt squeezed, and her pulse was racing. "You're not silver anymore."

"That is so." He inclined his head.

"I thought you couldn't get rid of the permapel without a special solvent."

"Even without applying the solvent, permapel starts to disintegrate after twenty-four hours of wear, and hot water considerably speeds the process. But you have no cause for alarm." Smiling slightly, Mac gestured to her father's baggy sweatpants. Except that on him they weren't baggy. "I have utilized the clothes you gave me to cover those parts of my body that embarrass you."

"Yes, I noticed that . . ."

"But you still seem to find my appearance shocking."

"Not shocking. You just look . . ." She swallowed hard. "You look different without the permapel."

"Perhaps we shall both get used to my new appearance eventually." His gaze held hers, and she saw a hint of color rise into his cheeks. He cleared his throat. "Since it's the custom of your time, I removed the permapel from my face as well as from my body. It seemed only practical if we are to avoid attracting attention. I hope you are not shocked, or offended."

"Offended? By seeing your face? N-no, of course not." She twitched nervously at her T-shirt, wishing she'd worn her snazzy yellow outfit, and still trying to come to terms with how incredibly good-looking Mac was without his layer of high-gloss silver.

With the permapel removed, his skin was a light brown color that took on an almost coppery hue against the ebony darkness of his hair. And his eyes! Ariel gulped. His blue eyes gleamed with a powerful intelligence that was readily apparent now that she wasn't seeing him through the distorting haze imparted by his silver skin. If he walked onto one of Miranda's movie sets, Ariel had no doubt he'd be hired on the spot, to add visual appeal, if for no other reason. He was, quite simply, gorgeous.

Mac squared his shoulders, visibly steeling himself to maintain direct eye contact with her. "In my time, it is considered a mark of special intimacy when people remove all covering from their faces. I realize this isn't true in your society, and that it's just a custom my culture has adopted over the last fifty years as permapel has become easier to apply and infinitely varied in patterns and colors. Still, I am finding that there is a great deal of power to everyday customs." He smiled wryly, stroking his cheek. "To be honest, Ariel, I feel as naked and embarrassed as you would feel if you displayed your body to me and to the world."

"Don't be embarrassed," Ariel said softly. "I'm glad to see the real you." She smiled shyly. "Your face looks very good when its naked."

"So does yours," he said, his voice husky. "You are a most beautiful woman, Ariel."

Hot color flooded her cheeks. This was crazy! If anyone had suggested yesterday that she would look at a man's face and experience a feeling of intimacy so intense it bordered on the erotic, she would have laughed out loud. But this was no joke, and she found that she couldn't look away. Her gaze settled with hypnotized fascination on Mac's mouth, and she realized with a thrill of shock that she was fantasizing about how it would feel if he kissed her.

Several seconds passed before she finally managed to tear her gaze away. She picked up the phone. "I have to call my sister," she said, dialing the number as she spoke. "Miranda will be worried sick. I must let her know I'm alive before we do anything else—"

"No," Mac said quickly. "Ariel, you haven't thought through the danger—"

"Hello," Ralph's voice said at the other end of the phone.

She smiled at the relief of hearing her brother-in-law's familiar voice, of being forced out of fantasy land and back into the normal, everyday world of the nineties. "Ralph, thank goodness you picked up the phone. This is—"

The receiver gave an ominous hiss and the phone went dead in her hand.

Ariel scowled. "Damn! Why do cheap phones always choose the worst moments to cause problems?" She slammed the useless receiver back into its cradle. "Excuse me, Mac, I need to use the phone in the living room. I've got to call Ralph right back. He'll be going crazy, wondering where I am and what happened to cut the connection."

"I cut the connection."

"What?"

"I cut the connection, or rather Pip did." Mac spoke quietly, but with unmistakable determination. "I'm sorry, Ariel, but I cannot allow you to speak to your sister or with Ralph, whoever he is. Not yet, when we have made no effort to plan for your safe escape. I hoped to convince the world that you died in the Pacific Ocean, but that may not be possible now that your neighbor has seen us come in here, and Ralph has heard your voice. However, you must not speak to him again and confirm that you are alive. Such an action is guaranteed to put you at tremendous risk."

Ariel decided not to point out that Ralph and Miranda had an automatic screening system on their phones that allowed them to identify their callers. Ralph almost certainly knew that the call came from her home before he answered the phone. Given that Ralph and the L.A. superintendent of police were good friends, it seemed likely that a posse of detectives would be knocking on her front door some time very soon. She realized, with only a small pang of guilty conscience, that she didn't want Mac to be with her, a prime target for arrest, when the police arrived.

She obviously needed to convince him that his worries about her safety were misplaced. "Mac, I appreciate your concern, really, but I'm sure Consuela is dead, so I'm going to be fine. You've got to stop worrying about me, and start thinking about yourself. I don't know what you have to do to get yourself back home to the twenty-second century, but whatever it is, I think you should start doing it real soon. I calculate that you have about fifteen minutes, tops, before the police get here to arrest you."

"Is that what you wish me to do, Ariel? Disappear? Vanish from your life, offering you my good wishes for the future and leaving you alone to face the consequences of my actions?"

She drew in a sharp, unexpectedly painful breath. "Yes, I guess that's what I want you to do, Mac. You belong in another world, and there's nothing but trouble waiting for you here in this one." Trying to ignore the dismay her own sensible suggestion provoked, she kept her smile pasted in place, even though it wobbled a bit. "I . . . I'm really pleased to have met you, Mac. These past few hours have been an extraordinary experience."

"An experience that is just beginning." Mac leaned forward so that the two of them were suddenly very close. "Now it's your turn to listen, Ariel, and to come out of your pleasant cocoon of delusion. Consuela is not dead. The medical technology of our time enables her to self-heal her wounds provided she was adequately prepared by our doctors with various emergency drugs and implants before she entered the time-travel chamber. It is just possible that she may still be in the deeply unconscious state that our self-healing process requires. Believe me, that state will last only another couple of hours, at best, and then she will be ready to pursue her plans. I have no idea what those plans may be, but you may be confident that they do not bode well for your world. You may also be confident that she has another identity already prepared, and she will not hesitate to annihilate you or anyone else who threatens the safety of that new identity."

He sounded so sure of himself that she almost began to believe him. "But, Mac, you saw all the blood last night! Consuela was scarcely breathing—"

"We don't have time to stand here arguing about whether Consuela is alive or dead," he said. "I am prepared to stake my future on the fact that she is alive, and that you are in grave danger. That's bad enough, but my whole world is in danger, which is even worse."

Something deep inside Ariel snapped. She had spent too much time as a child listening to her parents proclaim that the world would end if she continued to use hair spray, or eat red meat, or kill bugs with pesticide, or whatever happened to be their cause of the week. She refused to believe that the safety of Mac's civilization depended on the actions of a woman who had more than likely already bled to death. Civilization, it seemed to her, was not that fragile.

She muttered what was for her a violent swearword, and hopped past Mac into the living room, hating the fact that he moved with the speed and grace of a panther, while she scuttled around like a one-footed emu with arthritis. He'd already overtaken her before she could pick up the phone. She snatched it from him, and it went dead in her hand.

Furious, she pivoted around, mad enough to take a swing at him with her fist. Too late she remembered that only one of her ankles was in working order.

Mac caught her a split second before she stumbled over the telephone table, and Ariel made the shocking discovery that touching permapel and touching Mac's naked skin were two vastly different things. She would have moved away at once—wouldn't she?—except that moving too fast was what had precipitated this situation in the first place. So she stood very still, carefully not looking at him, feeling her skin begin to prick with a strange, tingling heat.

"Did you hurt yourself?" Mac asked, his voice gruff.

"No."

"That's good." He took a step forward, and somehow, she was standing within the circle of his arms, her head cradled against his chest, and Mac was stroking her hair in a steady, soothing rhythm. His skin felt warm beneath her cheek and now that he was no longer wearing permapel, she could hear the slow, strong beat of his heart. She had no idea why she suddenly started to tremble.

"Are you cold?" he asked.

"No." Her vocabulary seemed to have shrunk to monosyllables.

"Good." His hands moved up and down her spine, featherlight, infinitely beguiling. His thin cotton pants failed to disguise the fact that he was significantly aroused.

She wondered why she found the fact that Mac was aroused so intoxicating. She wondered why it felt so terrifyingly right to be held in his arms. She wondered if she really wanted to know the answers to her own questions.

"Mac, let me go," she whispered.

"Ariel, we must talk..."

Their voices came and died away in unison. He released his hold on her, leaving Ariel free to go where she pleased. But instead of moving away, she stayed right where she was.

Okay, so she might as well acknowledge the truth: she found Mac almost unbearably attractive. She tried to bring her usual common sense to bear. "I guess we're both getting turned on more by our situation than by anything else," she said with determined briskness. "This has been an extraordinary few hours for both of us and I expect we're translating other complicated emotions into something sexual."

"I'm sure you are right," Mac murmured, his hand cupping her face. "There is no logical reason for us to be sexually attracted to each other. You believe I'm crazy—"

"Our cultural differences are too great..."

"You wear nothing on your face and so I see every fleeting mood, every nuance of expression. That is why I find it so incredibly erotic to gaze at you." With tantalizing slowness, his head lowered toward her mouth. "That must be why I cannot stop imagining how it would taste to kiss you . . ."

He stopped moving toward her, his mouth no more than a breath away. Ariel tried to remember the point of what they'd been talking about, but all she could really think about was how badly she wanted Mac to kiss her. She waited for him to close the infinitesimal gap between his lips and hers, but he didn't move. The silence stretched between them, tense and freighted with emotion she didn't understand.

In the end, she was the one who linked her hands behind his head and brought his lips down to make contact with hers. His whole body tensed, as if in shock, and for an agonizing moment, she thought that he still might not kiss her. Then he made a harsh sound deep in his throat, and his mouth slanted across hers, hot and hungry with passion.

The kiss lasted no more than ten delirious, wonderful seconds. Then he broke away from her with devastating abruptness, swinging around so that his face was hidden from her.

"I cannot do this," he said, his voice husky and far from steady. "I apologize, Ariel, for taking from you something which you did not realize you were offering. In my world, a kiss exchanged between lovers is the ultimate act of passion, a gift of intimacy that we share only with the most special of partners. There are many promises implicit in the offer and acceptance of a kiss."

She struggled to get a hold of herself. "In my world, Mac, a kiss is just a kiss. You haven't taken anything I wasn't perfectly willing to give."

He turned back to her, just managing to smile. "It seems we have run smack into one of those cultural differences you were talking about, Ariel."

Sadly, she knew he was right. And the more time they spent together, the more likely it was that they would keep tripping over barriers and boundaries that one or the other of them didn't even know were there. She tried to return his smile, and couldn't quite make it, so she switched back to their old argument. "Mac, please ask Pip to fix my phones. I have to call my family, and you have to go home."

"You are wrong on both counts," he said. "You must not risk your safety, and you know that I can't return to my world until I have arrested Consuela Timmons."

"Mac, face facts. You have no chance of evading capture long enough to arrest Consuela Timmons. The police will be here at any minute. If you don't want to be arrested, tell Pip to take you home. Go back to your own time."

"You ask for a favor that I can't give," Mac said softly. "It is my sworn duty to find Consuela and take her back to stand trial."

"Well how in the world do you expect to do that?" she demanded.

He took her hands, cradling them between his. "I have no right to ask for your help, Ariel, but I believe the safety of my whole world and yours is at stake. I need you. Help me to function in your world without detection until I have found Consuela Timmons."

What he was asking was crazy, ridiculous, absurd and a dozen other similar adjectives. It was also intoxicatingly exciting. Still, Ariel knew she couldn't afford to get carried away. Since the day she left her parents' home for college, she'd dedicated her life to avoiding everything that was crazy, ridiculous, absurd. And exciting, a small voice whispered. Did you notice that you've ended up leading a life that's about as exciting as diet cookies?

She didn't have time to make a conscious decision about how she would answer Mac's plea. A thunderous knocking came at the door, and a hoarse masculine voice yelled through the steel panels.

"Ms. Hutton, are you in there? Open up, please, this is the police."

"Hmm, I do not believe we should speak with the police," Mac said. "I really do not think it would be a good idea." He held out his arms, and Ariel went into them with a willingness that ought to have shocked her. He bounded up the stairs into her bedroom and ran straight across to the French doors that led onto her balcony.

"There are no stairs down," Ariel warned him.

"Then we will go up."

The knocking grew louder. He opened the French doors and carried her outside, slamming them behind him.

He propped her against the wall, in deference to her sprained ankle, and jumped onto her ironwork table, springing from there onto the roof with such speed and agility that she barely saw him move. He leaned down.

"Quick," he said. "Now you give me your hands and I'll pull you up."

She could easily have screamed and attracted the attention of one of the cops milling below. Instead, she stretched up her arms, and he grasped her wrists, pulling her onto the roof alongside him. "Great," he said. "You are terrific, Ariel." He braced his feet on a chimney stack and tossed her over his shoulder, breaking into a run that seemed to pay no heed to the fact that the roof sloped at a forty-five-degree angle. Ariel looked down, and was rewarded with a heart-stopping view of the sidewalk and the police taking up positions around her town house.

She decided that she'd travel better if she kept her gaze fixed firmly at roof level. "Do you mind telling me where we're going?" she asked.

"As far as these roofs will take us."

"Mac, that isn't very far."

"So I see," he said, and if she hadn't known better, she would have sworn there was a trace of laughter in his voice. "You had better brace yourself, Ariel. I believe I shall have to jump."

"Jump where? What do you mean? Mac, there's nowhere to jump!"

He didn't answer. She felt his muscles bunch, and for a split second the speed of his run checked, and then he soared upward and outward into space.

Ariel closed her eyes and prepared to meet her end. This, she thought, is getting to be quite a habit.

5

MAC WAS off and running again almost before Ariel had time to register that they'd landed safely on the roof of the building next door. How in the world did he do it? she wondered. There must be at least six feet of empty space between one rooftop and the next, and he was burdened by carrying her. If he ever stopped running long enough for her to catch her breath, she'd have to ask him if he was an Olympic triathlon champion, or the twenty-second-century equivalent. Although the feats that Mac routinely accomplished seemed way beyond the range of even the most outstanding athlete.

She heard the wail of another approaching police siren and knew that however swiftly Mac leaped and ran, it could only be a matter of seconds before the police circled the buildings and ended up in a position to spot the pair of them. And Mac wouldn't be able to dodge bullets.

"Mac, we have to get off the roof," she panted. "The police will see us and one of them might get nervous and start shooting."

"You are right," he said. But instead of changing directions or scurrying about in search of cover, he simply speeded up his headlong dash toward the edge of the roof.

Ariel groaned, knowing that this time there was no new building for him to leap onto, only a frail-looking jacaranda tree and an alley that connected the utility court of her development to the parking lot of the strip mall next door.

"Oh, Lord, we're trapped," she said, her voice sounding hollow. "We're doomed." She clutched at Mac's arm. "You're going to be arrested for sure."

"I believe not—"

His calm was infuriating. "Mac, trust me, you're in big trouble."

"I will not allow you to be harmed, Ariel."

She clung to her fast-vanishing supply of patience. "Mac, you're the one who's in trouble! Whatever you do, don't tell the police that you're a time traveler, got that? Say you don't speak English, say you're an undocumented alien, say whatever you want—but not that you're from two hundred years in the future, okay?"

"Okay." He spoke the word musingly as he dodged a chimney stack. "Do you know that in Spanglish, we still use that word?"

"Mac!" she yelled. "This is not the time for an exchange of linguistic curiosities!"

"Okay, we will talk of more important things." He cast a brief, calculating glance toward the alley, then turned and smiled at her. "You do not think your police persons would be intrigued to learn that I have traveled back through two hundred years of time?"

She shuddered, visualizing the outcome of that conversation. "Trust me, Mac, they wouldn't be in the least interested because they wouldn't believe you. What they'd do is lock you up in a lunatic asylum—" She gasped, suddenly realizing from the flexing of his muscles and the coiled tension of his body that he'd been teasing her, and that he'd never had the slightest intention of turning himself in.

"Mac, good grief—you can't jump off the roof! My God, there's a twenty-foot drop to the ground! And it's not water when you land, it's concrete!" Concrete, with a lethal scattering of broken beer bottles around the large trash containers.

"I will go first," he said cheerfully, "and then you will jump after me. I will catch you." He smiled encouragingly, as if suggesting she might like to hop over a small puddle.

"Me?" she squeaked. "Jump off a building? Mac, you're nuts, totally and completely nuts. I can't jump twenty feet off a roof!"

"Of course you can. I am going now. You will come later." Mac eased her off his shoulders, sparing a couple of seconds to make sure that she was balanced securely in the roof gutter. Then he leaned forward at what Ariel considered a death-defying angle and grabbed the tip of the topmost branch of the jacaranda tree.

"Oh my God! Mac, that will never hold your weight! Don't do it!"

She was too late. Mac had already launched himself at the tree, using the slender branches more to break his fall than as actual supports. He slithered down the trunk, and collapsed for thirty or so agonizing seconds at its base in a clutter of leaves and blossoms. Then he jumped up, brushing his hands on the seat of his sweatpants, wincing only slightly.

"Okay," he said. "Your turn." He held up his arms and smiled encouragingly at Ariel.

He was, of course, certifiably crazy, but she knew that already. He seriously expected her to launch herself into his arms—over a twenty-foot drop. Ariel licked her bone-dry lips. Capture by the police was beginning to look better and better. "Mac, get real. I couldn't jump that far, even if my ankle was in perfect shape. I'll kill myself."

"I have already promised that I will catch you. Ariel, hurry up! We don't have time to argue. Listen, the police are right behind us."

Her stomach heaved with terror. "You can't possibly support my weight. We'll both be killed."

"Jump, Ariel," he said. "I am strong. Trust me. I can do it. You can do it."

If she did jump, it would be final, irrevocable proof that she'd lost her mind. Believing in time travel was nothing compared to believing she could take a twenty-foot leap off the top of a building and survive. She heard a sudden roar of voices approaching from behind her. The police. The people who would save her from Mac, not to mention her own sudden attack of madness. Any honest, sensible citizen would be rushing to turn herself in to the protective custody of the police.

Ariel half turned in the direction of the shouts. Then she turned back again to peer down at Mac. He smiled. God, he had the sexiest smile she'd ever seen in her life! No wonder her brains were mush.

"There she is, up on the roof! Hold it, miss, don't move!"

The voices sounded perilously near, barely yards away. It was now or never. She drew in a deep breath, closed her eyes, stretched out her arms and stepped out into space.

She landed with a bone-jarring thump in Mac's arms, and her foot bounced against the pavement, sending excruciating pain shooting briefly through her sprained ankle. He staggered at the impact, but quickly righted himself.

When she risked opening her eyes, he was looking down at her, his eyes very bright, his arms feeling strong and oddly comforting as they held her. Her stomach gave a weird little somersault that had nothing whatsoever to do with the fact that she'd just survived a suicidal jump off a roof with all her body parts intact.

Mac grinned at her, his gaze warm with approval. He jiggled her arm experimentally. "All limbs still safely attached to the torso, it seems. You see, I knew you could do it."

Ariel decided it was the ridiculous rush of adrenaline to her head that prevented her from coming up with some suitably scathing comment, and shock that caused her legs to feel weak and shaky. It had nothing to do with Mac's smile. If he hadn't whipped her up into his arms and dodged behind a garbage container, she'd have pointed out that they had no realistic chance of escaping the swarms of police who must have seen her jump and would soon fan out to search the area. But since he was already running again, she decided to save her breath. There wasn't much point in talking to a man who was deaf to good sense.

Mac broke out from the cover of the container and made a beeline for the shopping-center parking lot. "Is your foot really okay?" he asked. "Can you drive?"

He was going to steal another car. Oh, Lord! Why did he keep forcing her to become an accomplice to his crimes? Except, of course, that he wasn't really forcing her. Much as she would like to pretend otherwise, Ariel knew she'd had a dozen opportunities to escape from Mac if she'd really wanted to. Since she'd taken none of them, she could only conclude that she'd absorbed more of her parents' casual attitude toward the law than she'd ever have imagined possible. The shocking truth was that, far from being coerced, she was actively helping Mac to escape from the police.

She drew in a shaky breath, trying to come to terms with the knowledge that she was as much a fugitive from the law as he was. "My ankle's fine. I can drive," she said tersely.

"That is very good." He gave her a smile of such warm approval, for a moment her stupid heart seemed to stop beating. She scowled to cover her confusion, but Mac didn't see because he was making a dash for the closest car and instructing Pip to unlock the doors as he ran.

Mac shoved her behind the wheel of a blue GM Saturn and sprang into the passenger seat. Pip turned on the ignition, giving a self-satisfied little hiccup when the engine fired at the first attempt.

"Get us out of here, Ariel!" Mac ordered. "Pip indicates that the nearest police persons are only two hundred meters away."

"Where am I supposed to go?" she asked, backing out of the parking space at high speed, and narrowly avoiding a cruising Mustang.

"Drive us toward your sister's home. I assume Consuela was taken to a medical facility near the place in which her injury occurred. If we are very lucky, I might find her still in the hospital."

Ariel was too busy driving to point out for the umpteenth time that Consuela was dead. Mac looked over his shoulder and aimed Pip toward the rear window. The computer spat out a stream of liquid, incomprehensible words.

"If Pip is right, the police persons have lost track of us," Mac said. "They're looking for dead bodies, fortunately. Go quickly, Ariel, so that they don't pick up a tail on us."

Too many more of these high-speed chases, and she'd be a genuine dead body, Ariel thought. At the very least, she'd need a heart transplant. A woman of her orderly disposition wasn't equipped for accelerating through intersections and burning rubber down the access ramp onto the freeway. Until yesterday, her definition of high adventure had been painting her toenails Sinfully Scarlet. Now she was on the lam, in cahoots with a time traveler and chasing a presidential assassin. Her situation was so absurd, her nerves should have been shredded. Strangely, her nerves seemed quite fine. In fact, her entire system seemed to be energized.

"Have we still lost them?" she asked Mac, when they'd been driving for a while without the wail of a single siren to distract them.

"I think so. I can't see any police vehicles, and Pip is issuing no warnings." He rubbed his hand across his eyes, and she noticed his face was stark white beneath its tan.

"What's the matter?" she asked.

"It is . . . nothing of consequence."

"Yes, it is. Are you hurt? Did you injure yourself when you made one of those crazy jumps?"

"No." His voice sounded thick. "I am . . . tired, that is all. I have drawn heavily on my reserves of energy today. The metabolism of the human body has been genetically enhanced over the past few generations so that our endurance is much greater and our energy levels higher than yours. Also our ability to jump high, run fast and swim for many hours. But to compensate, when our bodies reach a serious state of overexertion, we are afflicted with a fatigue so powerful that we feel it as pain."

"Then sleep," she said. "I'm driving the car, and I know where I'm going. There's nothing all that important for you to do at the moment." She smiled faintly. "Recoup your energies for the next time you need to leap tall buildings in a single bound."

He spoke quietly. "And if I sleep, Ariel, where will I find myself when I wake up?"

She drew in a sharp breath, shocked to realize that he was worried in case she turned him in to the police. It was a measure of how far she'd traveled emotionally in the last few hours that she felt hurt by his lack of faith in her integrity. "You've asked me several times to trust you," she said stiffly. "I guess you'll have to decide whether you're willing to do the same with me. I plan to take us to a motel, where we can both rest and regroup for a couple of hours. We can't make a sensible plan for dealing with Consuela if we have to keep running. We need somewhere to sit and think."

He looked at her for a long, silent moment. Then, without speaking, he leaned back in the seat and closed his eyes. Within thirty seconds, he was deeply asleep. When Mac decided to give his trust, it seemed that he gave it completely.

The highway was plastered with plenty of advertisements for nearby motels, but Ariel didn't want to pull off the road before she'd put several more miles between themselves and the Laguna Hills police. Fortunately, traffic was light, and after driving for half an hour, she felt safe enough to start looking for the sort of cheap, clean, anonymous motel where the desk clerk wasn't likely to ask awkward questions.

She was about to turn off the highway in pursuit of a promising motel, when she suddenly remembered that cheap wouldn't cut it as far as she and Mac were concerned. Dread squeezed the breath out of her lungs when she registered the fact that they were flat broke. Good Lord, how could she have forgotten such an important fact? When the police pounded on the door of her town house, Mac had whisked her away so fast that she hadn't given her wallet a single thought, much less stopped to grab it. She didn't have a credit card or a dollar to her name, and Mac probably had never seen real money, except in a museum display. He certainly wasn't carrying any 1996 dollars tucked in his sweatpants. Even if she found the perfect motel to hide in for a few hours, they couldn't pay for a room, or even a candy bar from the lobby vending machine. As far as she could see, the pair of them had no hope of buying food, clothing or shelter any time in the near future.

She hadn't noticed how hungry she was until she knew that they had no money to buy food. A brush of genuine panic feathered Ariel's spine. What could they do? How were they going to keep running when they had no funds to smooth their escape route?

The answer came almost at once. They couldn't, it was that simple. Either they acquired some money, or they stopped running. And stopping running was tantamount to Mac's agreeing to turn himself in—and by this time, her own record wouldn't be looking too rosy. Unless Ralph was kind enough to provide her with a fancy, high-priced lawyer, she was going to find herself locked up in a small room with no view.

She wrestled with this intractable problem as she drove north, circling the area where Consuela might have been taken to the hospital. Eventually, she decided that these were problems she shouldn't even try to resolve on her own, since the final decision to surrender had to be Mac's. While he slept, her task was to keep them both safe from police scrutiny. She'd given him her word, and she believed in keeping promises once you made them.

The Saturn, fortunately, had plenty of gas, and—in view of the grim state of their finances—driving around for an hour or so was probably the easiest way to keep him out of sight of marauding cops.

Her stomach growled hungrily as she passed a few fast-food restaurants. She sighed, and tried to tell herself that fasting for a few hours was a great way to start losing the five pounds she'd been planning to diet away ever since last Christmas.

Mac was still deeply asleep, his slow, shallow breathing causing a barely perceptible rise and fall of his chest. His face looked sterner, older and a lot more intimidating without the humorous gleam in his eyes to soften his expression. A formidable man, Ariel found herself thinking, even when cast adrift in a world that was totally unfamiliar to him. She'd be sorry to see him return to his own time; there were so many questions she would have liked to ask him, so many intriguing discussions that they hadn't been able to have. Even if

Mac hadn't been chasing a presidential assassin from two hundred years in the future, she had a feeling he'd still be one of the most exciting men she'd ever met.

The irate honk of a horn drew Ariel's attention back to the road, reminding her that the California highway system was not a safe place to daydream. She switched on the radio, flipping buttons until she reached an all-news station, hoping to hear what line the media were taking in reporting the story of her kidnapping and Consuela's murder.

She caught the end of a local weather forecast which predicted no disasters of flood, fire or sliding earth. A good day for the battered state of California.

At the top of the hour, the station repeated the day's major headlines. Congress was getting ready to slash more funds from the national budget; another deadly skirmish in the former Yugoslavia had killed five children; and a radical religious group had accused the British and Irish governments of lack of good faith in negotiating the future of Northern Ireland.

All in all, Ariel concluded, Mac's rupture of the time barrier didn't seem to be having much impact on the conduct of world affairs. People were behaving with their usual depressing lack of compassion and good sense.

The voice of the newsreader changed from brisk-male to cheerful, low-pitched female. "I'm Mary Christine Kelly, and in local news, police continue to investigate the disappearance of Ariel Hutton, whose TV documentaries have won her two Emmy nominations and a position as senior producer at our local PBS affiliate.

"In a startling development, Brenda Lewinski, a neighbor and friend of Ms. Hutton, claims to have been attacked and left for dead inside Ariel Hutton's town house in Laguna Hills. Brenda was knocked unconscious by a tall, silver-skinned man who appeared to be on friendly terms with Ms. Hutton.

"In response to numerous questions, Police Superintendent Costello stuck to the official line that there is as yet no conclusive physical evidence that Ariel Hutton survived last night's suicidal leap into the Pacific Ocean. When asked about reports that numerous civilian employees at Camp Pendleton Marine Corps base claim to have seen Ms. Hutton and her silver-skinned companion, Superintendent Costello refused to comment. He also refused to comment on the report that Ms. Hutton escaped arrest a short while ago by jumping off the twenty-foot-high roof of the building next door to her town house."

A definite trace of amusement entered Mary Christine's voice. "Police are justifying their caution by pointing out that they've been swamped with reports of alien invaders abducting local women. Sightings of naked, silver-skinned men have been coming in from all across the Greater Los Angeles Area. When questioned, most of these aliens turn out to be college students trying to win bets. So far, thirteen arrests for drunk and lewd public behavior have been made. However, in an interesting twist, according to information supplied to reporters by Brenda Lewinski, the man who attacked her was not naked. She described him as wearing yellow flowered pants topped by a woman's pink, semitransparent polyester blouse. She also claimed that his facial features were— quote—violent and brutal—and that he had piercing coal-black eyes."

"What!" Ariel stared in disgust at the radio. Trust Brenda to exaggerate. "Violent and brutal? Good grief, woman, he was as polite as could be when he met you! And he has blue eyes, for your information."

Still, perhaps she should be grateful for her neighbor's exaggerations. Life would be much easier for her and Mac if false reports about his appearance continued to circulate. She listened intently as Mary Christine reported the approaching release from County Memorial Hospital of Consuela Timmons, the woman "viciously attacked and left for dead just prior to the disappearance of Ariel Hutton and her mysterious silver-painted friend."

"Friend?" Ariel muttered in astonishment. "Hey, wait a minute! Didn't anyone notice I was kidnapped? What about a word of sympathy for me? I was a victim, too, you know."

"Ms. Timmons had lost copious amounts of blood prior to her arrival at the hospital," the newscaster continued. "However, Dr. Simon Brody, chief of surgery at Memorial, reports that her wounds are much less severe than originally thought, and it's expected that Ms. Timmons will be fit enough to return to her home in Sacramento within the next twenty-four hours."

Her home in Sacramento? Did Consuela have documentation to explain her presence here? Ariel wondered. Had Mac been correct in claiming that she was well prepared for her escape back in time?

Mary Christine's chirpy voice was beginning to get on Ariel's nerves, but a final snippet of news caught her attention. "Miranda Hutton, sister to Ariel, and star of the recent hit movie, *Night City,* is reportedly sedated and under the care of her physician. Ralph Dunnett, Miranda's husband, issued a statement saying that he and his wife refuse to believe that Ariel had anything to do with the attack on Consuela Timmons, and that they are both praying for the swift and safe return of their sister."

Ariel stared in stupefied silence at the radio, even her worry about letting Miranda know she was alive fading in the light of the stunning spin that was obviously being put on her disappearance.

Ralph and Miranda didn't believe she had anything to do with the attack on Consuela Timmons.

The only reason Ariel could think of for Ralph to protest her innocence was that the police suspected her of being Mac's accomplice. And while it might be true that she'd helped Mac today, it certainly hadn't been true last night. At least four people had witnessed Mac grab her as a hostage. They must have heard her scream, seen her struggle. Why hadn't they told the police she'd been kidnapped? Was it possible that Miranda's guests had been so drunk, they hadn't been able to give a coherent account of what had happened?

With a chill of foreboding, Ariel realized that neither the giant rabbits, nor the angel and devil, had arrived on the scene until the very moment that Consuela jerked her throat against the blade of Mac's knife. They had no way of knowing that Ariel was the woman who'd screamed for help, no way of knowing that Consuela had tried to kill Mac. Coming as they did upon the scene, they might have assumed that Consuela was the one calling out, and that Mac slit her throat in an effort to silence her.

In fact, looking back, Ariel realized just how false an impression the four party-goers might have gotten. It was conceivable, she supposed, that it had never occurred to anyone that Mac was kidnapping her. Mac had waved his knife around and warned the bystanders to keep back, so she'd assumed they would all realize what was going on. In retrospect, she could see how easily Mac's actions might have been misunderstood.

She snapped off the radio, too tense to listen to other news. Good grief, what an unholy mess! The police, far from considering her the innocent and abused victim of a kidnapping, probably had a warrant out for her arrest! Ariel gulped, and wondered if she was going to throw up. She hadn't even gotten a parking ticket since she graduated from college ten years ago, and now she was the prime suspect in a case of attempted murder.

The idea of boring, uptight, pay-your-taxes-a-month-in-advance Ariel Hutton being a wanted criminal was so absurd, she ought to be laughing. In all honesty, she thought suddenly, there was a kind of strange, secret excitement knowing that she was on the run from the law. If it weren't for the fact that Miranda and Ralph must be out of their minds with worry, she had a suspicion she might actually be enjoying herself.

But Miranda and Ralph *were* worried, and Ariel couldn't just leave her sister in total ignorance of what was going on. She knew from too many painful childhood experiences how terrifying it was to be worried about the safety of people you loved. As a practical matter, however, she had no idea how to get in touch with Miranda without bringing the police running hotfoot in pursuit. By now, her sister's phones would be bugged, which ruled out making a phone call, and a personal visit was out of the question. She and Mac might be able to evade the police and wend their way back to Miranda's house after dark, but Ralph had a state-of-the-art electronic security system that triggered if you so much as breathed on it. By the time she and Mac walked up the front path, they would have tripped enough alarms to wake up the entire state of California, let alone the local police.

Ariel drove around for another forty minutes, trying to think of some way to get in touch with Miranda and Ralph. She'd come up with nothing even remotely useful, when Mac woke up as abruptly as he'd fallen asleep, with only a few seconds between unconsciousness and total alertness.

He straightened in his seat, his body radiating energy, the hard planes and angles of his face softened by his immediate smile.

"Hi."

"Hi." Ariel felt herself smiling back. "You look a lot better, Mac."

"Thanks to you, I feel a lot better. Almost normal, in fact, and ravenously hungry."

Her stomach rumbled at the reminder. "Unfortunately, there's not much we can do about that. We have no money, and no credit cards. Without money, we can't eat, pay for a motel room or even put gas in this car. That's why we're still driving around."

He pulled a face. "Money! I should have remembered we would need it. Damn!"

"How do you pay for the things you buy?" she asked. "You must need some form of credit card. Not that it would do us any good even if you'd brought it with you."

He shook his head. "No cards. In my time, we use a retinal scan for identification when we conduct any business transaction. Earlier on, I was congratulating myself on the fact that in the twentieth century you still use paper money, so nobody would be able to trace us when we made a purchase. I neglected to worry about the fact that we have none."

The snippets of information he dropped about the organization of his world didn't sound all that wonderful to Ariel. "Don't you ever yearn for the privacy to do something without having it show up on the official record?" she asked.

"Sometimes. We are aware of the freedoms we have given up in the name of social tranquillity and personal safety. But I think there are few people in our time who would trade your sense of privacy for our sense of security. The Great Famine taught us that freedom has no meaning if it brings only the freedom to die."

The Great Famine really didn't sound as if it was going to be a nice time in which to live, but for the moment, at least, Ariel decided she was too busy taking care of the present to worry about how she was going to save the future. "Since retinal scans don't work for us, Mac, the bottom line is that we're soon going to be stranded. I estimate we can go about another thirty miles in this car before we run out of gas. And I really think we have to stop stealing cars as a solution to our problems. I reckon we've already run up about a thousand dollars' worth of car damage that I'm going to have to pay back some time."

Mac frowned, his forehead wrinkling in thought. "How do the people of your time get money when they need it?"

"First, we have to earn it. Then we write a check, or we put a plastic card into an automatic money machine—"

"Wait! How does your card system work? Is it electronic? Computer controlled?"

"Well, yes, but I don't have my bank card with me—"

"That is no problem." He smiled cheerfully. "Pip will be able to access the system and remove as much money as you wish. Your computers are so primitive, it's very easy for Pip to bypass their security codes."

"Hallelujah!" Ariel breathed, taking the insult to twentieth-century computers in stride. The thought that she might be able to eat again within the foreseeable future was enough to make her feel positively benevolent. On the point of heading the car toward the nearest bank-teller machine, she reluctantly concluded that she ought to tell Mac the news about Consuela Timmons first.

"I heard a report on the radio about Consuela," she said. "It seems she was taken to County Memorial Hospital for treatment, and they're about to release her. I've been heading in the direction of the hospital ever since I heard the news bulletin. We're only a couple of minutes away right now."

"That is most excellent detective work, Ariel." Mac was tactful enough not to point out that he'd been right all along about Consuela Timmons surviving her slashed throat, and Ariel refrained from pointing out that listening to the radio was not exactly genius-level investigative procedure. Mac leaned forward in the seat, his body radiating tension. "I hope to God we get there in time for me to arrest her," he said.

Ariel turned off the exit ramp and followed the signs for the main hospital entrance. "Mac, I'm bringing us here because I knew you'd want to come and I don't have any better ideas. But you can't just march up to Consuela's bedside and slap a pair of handcuffs on her, you know. We need to have some sort of a plan here. For a start, this is a huge place. We're going to have a lot of trouble locating her and we can't risk wandering around for too long, asking questions. People will get suspicious, not about Consuela, but about us. About you."

"I shall be able to locate Consuela." He touched his Pip. "Remember, this was a Silver Ceremony gift from President Timmons, which means that Consuela's retinal I.D. is already inserted into its data banks. I can locate her anywhere within a fifty-kilometer radius."

Ariel wasn't sure whether to be impressed or appalled by the thought of partners being able to keep a constant check on each other's whereabouts. Still, at this precise moment, the fact that Mac could track Consuela within the confines of the hospital was a major plus and she could debate the social wisdom of it later.

"Pip should be able to scan the entire hospital for Consuela before we even get out of the car," she said, pleased.

Mac hesitated for a moment. "I would prefer to scan when we are inside the hospital," he said.

"Why?"

"If Consuela happens to have her Pip with her, it might be programmed to alert her when she is scanned. I would prefer that she has the minimum time in which to take evasive action."

"You mean that there's going to be a struggle before you manage to take her into custody, don't you?"

"I trust not," Mac said. "Come, Ariel, let us not delay any longer. If you lean on my arm, can you walk?"

"Shuffle, anyway." She stepped out of the car, slamming the door behind her. Suddenly, she tossed her head back and laughed, stretching her arms wide. "No purse, no car keys, nothing except the police hot on my tail. You know, it's kind of a liberating sensation to be totally without possessions." She was appalled when she heard what she'd said. Good grief, what had happened to concepts like responsibility, and duty and common sense?

Mac gave a quick smile and held out his hand. "I shall remind you of that next time you complain because we're running across a rooftop a scant few meters ahead of the police."

It was probably an attack of light-headedness brought on by lack of food, but for a second Ariel found herself thinking that running across rooftops wasn't such a bad way to spend time, provided you had Mac as your partner. She didn't say anything, of course. He held his arm steady beneath hers, and she hopped and shuffled to the entrance of the hospital.

Once inside, Mac avoided eye contact with people they passed by pretending to carry on an intense conversation with her, but she could see that his attention was riveted by the sights and sounds of the busy hospital. Paramedics rushed along the corridor with a patient almost submerged beneath tubes, drips, IVs and portable monitors, and Mac paled.

"What is it?" she asked, low voiced. "Was that Consuela? Did you recognize her beneath all that equipment?"

He shook his head. "No, I didn't recognize that patient."

"You looked shocked."

He hesitated a moment before replying. "I reacted because I'm not accustomed to seeing people suffering so acutely."

"People in your time must get ill, surely. And accidents must happen even in the future."

"Freak accidents happen, yes, but rarely. Our society would not tolerate the dangers that you consider commonplace."

Ariel found that comment rather funny, given that the guy had hurtled back through time only the night before, and then had proceeded to throw himself off a cliff, leap across rooftops and generally create mayhem. "What do we tolerate that's so dangerous?" she asked.

"War, crime, poverty, violence." He smiled faintly. "Automobiles."

"And you don't have any of those things?" she asked incredulously. "No poverty? No crime?"

"Certainly no automobiles," he said. "And we have had no war in over a hundred years. As for crime and violence, even in your time, sociologists have shown that violent behavior is linked closely to poverty, so since we have no poverty, we have very little crime."

"Wait a minute," Ariel said. "That sounds very neat, but if you don't have any crime in your society, how come you're back here in the 1990s, chasing an assassin who killed your president? Doesn't murder count as kind of a major crime for a society that's not supposed to have any such thing?"

"It most certainly does," he said grimly. "And I said we have *little* crime, not that we have none. Unfortunately, it seems that in every generation there are a few people who choose to become criminals, despite society's best efforts at education and rehabilitation. That's why we have a United Bureau of Criminal Investigation, and why I have a job as its director. But the murder of President Timmons seems all the more terrible to our people because violence is so rare, and because we have so many other, lawful ways in which Consuela could have expressed her frustration with the policies of President Timmons."

Ariel would have liked to ask which of the president's policies Consuela had disagreed with so strongly that she'd felt the urge to kill her own sister, but they'd reached the elevator banks at the center of the hospital and they were surrounded by too many people to start such an outlandish conversation.

"Surgical patients are on the fourth floor," she said, reading the sign. She reached up and spoke softly into Mac's ear. "You'd better start scanning for Consuela's precise location. So that we know where she is before we arrive on her floor."

The elevator arrived and the doors slid open, disgorging a crowd of nurses, medical technicians and visitors. Taking advantage of the momentary confusion, Mac issued a soft-voiced instruction to Pip, who responded with a string of liquid-sounding commentary.

Apparently, whatever Pip had said infuriated Mac. His eyes darkened, his lips tightened into a grim, slashing line and he uttered a short, pithy expletive that Ariel was quite glad not to understand. He grabbed Ariel around the waist and shouldered his way out past a woman carrying a basket of blood samples.

"Stay here!" he ordered Ariel, dumping her into the first available chair and breaking into a run that was fast enough to turn heads. "Don't move, okay?"

Ariel didn't answer. There was no way she could hope to catch up with him, especially with her injured ankle, but she sure as heck didn't plan to sit in a plastic chair twiddling her thumbs, waiting for him to come back. Ariel hobbled in Mac's wake, falling farther and farther behind, until the corridor dead-ended in a set of heavy-duty fire doors. She pushed them open with some difficulty and stepped out onto the concrete landing too late to see whether he'd gone up or down.

She heard the faintest thud of rapid footsteps coming from a flight of stairs at least three floors down, followed by the distant slam of a heavy door. Mac? Consuela? Ariel stood clutching the stair rail, trying to decide whether her ankle would survive the climb downstairs, when the fire door that led to the second floor banged open. A tall, slender woman hurtled through, rushing for the stairs, her throat dramatically bandaged in stark white, and her long dark hair streaming out behind her.

Consuela, Ariel thought. And then, My God, she's so beautiful!

A second later, Mac reappeared, a floor lower than Consuela. She must have known he was there, although she didn't waste time looking over her shoulder. She ran up the stairs so rapidly that her sneakered feet barely seemed to land on any individual step. Mac followed behind, visibly gaining on Consuela, taking the stairs two at a time. It could only be a matter of moments before he caught up with her.

Mac yelled something, but the echoes of the stairwell made it hard to hear exactly what he'd said, and Ariel wasn't sure whether he'd spoken to her or Consuela. She decided that discretion was the better part of valor. Her physical strength was puny—laughable—in comparison to Consuela's and Mac's, so she'd be of most help if she kept out of the way. She flattened herself against the stair rail and prepared to watch Consuela race past.

But Consuela didn't race past. Instead, she executed a swift sidestep off the stairs, and, moving with the grace of a ballerina, lunged toward Ariel. Before Ariel could even gather her wits, much less escape, Consuela pivoted on the ball on her left foot and delivered a swinging karate-style kick to Ariel's ribs.

The blow was punishing in its power and astonishingly painful in its impact. Ariel doubled over, retching, watching scarlet stars explode in front of her eyes. Even as she collapsed, gasping for breath, Consuela grabbed her by the hair and tossed her into Mac's path. Ariel hit Mac's chest with a force that stopped him dead in his tracks, and knocked the pair of them into a sprawling heap on the concrete floor.

Consuela didn't wait to crow her triumph, or even to glance at what she'd wrought. She turned and fled through the fire doors, leaving Mac trapped beneath Ariel's limp and aching body.

He pushed her aside, for once not even bothering to ask if she was hurt. He came to his feet running.

The last thing she saw before she blacked out was Mac, dashing through the fire doors, in hot pursuit of Consuela.

6

HIS AWARD as incompetent dumbass of the year was in the bag, Mac thought gloomily, bursting through the fire doors onto the busy second floor of the hospital. He sidestepped a man in a green face mask, doubled back around a trolley piled high with linens and finally had a clear view of the hospital corridor.

Consuela was nowhere to be seen, of course, and Pip couldn't tell him a damn thing about her whereabouts because she was blocking all retinal probes, no doubt using a Pip equipped with an illegal scan-buster. She must have had the device inserted as a subdermal implant, so that she would never lose it. By now, she was probably well on the way to whatever bolt hole she'd prepared for herself, laughing all the way.

Mac bit back a violent oath, his emotions raw, his gut aching. Yeah, sweet, earnest, shy Consuela had thought of everything. Including details like making sure that the nation's top cop never noticed that his promised Silver Partner was planning to murder the president. She'd worked real hard to ensure that he was so caught up in plans for impending fatherhood that he never inquired too closely into the activities of the woman who was promising to bear his longed-for daughter.

He searched the corridor with grim determination and minimal hope, and came up with nothing. Life in the twenty-second century was carefully crafted to be both peaceful and emotionally restful. His job had made Mac hard and cynical in comparison to his fellow citizens, but neither his cynicism nor his professional training had prepared him for the events of the past twenty-four hours. Since the murder of President Timmons, he'd experienced more anger, more confusion and more bewilderment than at any other period of his life.

And not only because of Consuela's multiple betrayals. Ariel Hutton was the most unsettling woman he'd ever encountered, far more complex than Consuela, whose hunger for power might be despicable, but was at least easy to understand. Ariel, Mac decided, was an altogether more mysterious being.

He gave a ferocious scowl as he remembered that he'd left her passed out on the steps of the fire escape. He'd better go and find her before she recovered consciousness and decided to do something totally crazy like—God knew what. Where Ariel and trouble were concerned, his imagination failed him.

He strode back down the corridor and pushed open the heavy safety doors, deriving a childish satisfaction from letting them bang shut behind him. Hell, he had good reason to be angry. His own stupidity might have helped Consuela escape the first time, but he wasn't responsible for this new debacle. No, he knew precisely where to lay the blame for Consuela's latest escape, and it was right at the infuriating feet of Ariel Hutton. If Ariel had stayed in the damn chair as she was asked, Consuela wouldn't have managed to escape for a second time in the space of twenty-four hours.

Mac's sense of injury grew. No more Mr. Nice Guy, he decided. He would make it clear to Ariel that when he gave orders, she was to follow them. To the letter. No questions asked. Dammit, he was the director of the United Bureau of Criminal Investigation! His position ought to count for something, even in the backward society of the 1990s.

Mac stomped across the dusty concrete landing to the steps where Ariel still lay curled in a limp, self-protective ball. He looked down at her, and his scowl vanished. God, how frail she looked, how heartbreakingly vulnerable. Her face wasn't simply pale, it was frost-white. A trickle of blood had seeped out of a cut on her forehead, drying in a thin brown crust. Her eyes were shut, and he couldn't see any sign that she was breathing.

Seized by fear, Mac could barely swallow over the sudden lump in his throat, and his voice was thick when he instructed Pip to scan for injuries. Pip's power cell pulsed in a rainbow of refracted light as it gave its report: Ariel Hutton was free of life-threatening trauma; she was, however, suffering from a minor concussion, three cracked ribs, superficial bruises and a general state of exhaustion. All this, in addition to her sprained ankle, which Pip had no way to heal.

Mac couldn't begin to imagine the discomfort Ariel's primitive body must be experiencing with such an extensive list of injuries and no internal mechanism for healing them. The first-aid program on his Pip was limited, but it could easily perform a task as simple as mending bone. Mac gave Pip the order to repair Ariel's cracked ribs, then sat on the steps to wait for the laser fusion to be complete.

He was acutely aware of his own weariness after too brief a rest and not enough food, and his skin cells were no longer filtering out awareness of changes in temperature and humidity. He noticed how cool the concrete felt now that his systems were down and he wasn't protected by his usual layer of permapel. In this new world, all sensations seemed more intense and more immediate. Why else did his heart get this odd squeezing sensation every time he thought about Ariel? Why else did it seem so hard to breathe when he looked down at her and saw the beam of laser light tracing a slow, healing path over her injuries?

Pip reported Ariel's cracked ribs repaired. Mac pulled her into his arms, cradling her against his chest, and rocking gently back and forth as he ordered Pip to adjust the bio-rhythms of her body into a swifter healing mode. He felt a strange surge of protectiveness when Pip completed the adjustment and she began to stir, moaning as she struggled back to consciousness.

Mac wondered how it was possible to feel irritation, protectiveness and desire all at the same time, and all toward the same woman. Ever since he'd traveled back in time, he seemed to have been infected with the messy emotions of the people around him, and he had no idea how to handle them. He wasn't used to feeling sexual desire for a woman he scarcely knew. Like most men in the twenty-second century, he'd enjoyed a succession of gratifying sexual relationships with agreeable women. His partners had all been his friends before they became bedmates, and they remained friends when the sexual relationship ended. His desire for sex, like theirs, had been straightforward, open and uncomplicated, a pleasant aspect of friendship.

The concept of feeling intense desire for a woman who simultaneously annoyed the hell out of him seemed almost kinky by the standards with which he'd been raised. Yet what he was feeling now was unquestionably desire and he had the erection to prove it. All in all, Mac decided, pushing a strand of soft, light brown hair off Ariel's forehead, she was turning out to be a very confusing woman, and he had no idea why he felt this crazy longing to be close to her, to win her approval, to see her smile at him with unshadowed happiness.

She finally opened her eyes and stared at him groggily. Then her gaze focused and she licked her dry, cracked lips. "Where's Consuela?" she mumbled. "Didn't you catch her?"

Didn't he catch her? So much for winning Ariel's approval. He took a deep, calming breath. "No, I didn't catch her," he said, managing with considerable difficulty not to shout.

"Where is she, then? Why didn't you catch her? Did you chase her?"

"Yes, I chased her." Mac's temper, normally under perfect control, snapped. "But thanks to you, I have no idea where she has gone. Maybe if you had stayed where I asked you to stay, she would be safely in my custody be now and en route to trial before the High Court of my country—"

"If you'd told me what you were doing, instead of running off like a madman—"

"I told you Consuela was dangerous, which should have been enough to ensure that you would stay where I put you! But no! You had to come running after me, putting yourself in harm's way, endangering both of us." Mac realized he was yelling, an unforgivable piece of rudeness in his society. He subsided into abrupt silence, appalled by his own lapse of basic good manners.

Ariel merely glowered at him. "I'm not a package you can dump for later pickup. I was trying to take care of you!"

Mac's resolutions about not losing his cool flew straight out the window. "You? Take care of me? Hah! Be grateful that Consuela was more interested in escaping from me than in killing you. Otherwise, woman, I can guarantee that by now you would be dead!"

"I hate it when you call me woman in that tone of voice!"

"'Woman' is a term of respect in my society!"

"But you're here, in my time, remember? And here it sounds rude and patronizing!" Hot angry color flooded Ariel's cheeks. She pushed weakly at Mac's arms and he let her go, alarmed by the strength of his desire to hold on to her, to subdue her, to use his superior strength to bend her to his will. Good God, he'd never experienced such primitive, uncivilized urges before and he found them totally disconcerting.

She dragged herself up, clutching the stair rail to prevent herself from keeling over again. "Don't take out your wounded macho pride on me, Mac! It's not my fault your former girlfriend has managed to outwit you every step of the way."

He sprang to his feet. "Consuela would never outwit me in normal circumstances. She has prepared herself to live in this time. I have not!"

"That's obvious," Ariel snapped. "She's running rings around you at the moment, that's for sure." She swayed as she spoke, and Mac took a quick step forward, reaching out to grab her arm before she could do herself another injury. She cringed away from him, her face expressing a flash of sudden fear.

God in heaven, she was frightened of him! Mac stared at her in horror. After spending all these hours with him, how could she still believe he was capable of inflicting intentional harm? He might have felt the urge to subdue her, but he'd resisted the impulse. He never would have abused his physical strength in such a despicable way.

"Ariel, do not look at me so!" he said huskily. "Surely you know by now that I could never hurt you."

For a moment, he thought he saw the sheen of tears in her eyes. "I'm exhausted," she said. "I'm scared and I'm hungry, and I think I'm turning into my mother. I don't know anything anymore."

He took her into his arms, pulling her close, not even sure why he needed to hold her. He knew only that her tears lacerated him, and that his arms felt cold and empty without her. She resisted for a moment, holding herself stiff and unyielding in his embrace. Years of careful training in sexual sensitivity had taught him that he ought to let her go instantly, at the first sign of resistance. But he was desperate to make her understand—to have her feel—how important she was becoming to him and how much he cared about her well-being. He couldn't bear the idea of letting her go.

He buried his face in the soft, tangled mass of her hair and breathed in the old-fashioned apple scent of the shampoo she'd used that morning. His hands caressed her, his touch gentle and respectful, trying to show her how much he cared about her, how much he wanted to be her friend.

Slowly, she relaxed against him, and he felt the tremor of her response when he pulled her closer. To his dismay, he felt himself grow hard, but Ariel didn't reject him, and he let his erection press against her belly. He stroked his hand up and down her spine, expertly seeking out her pleasure spots, manipulating her reactions, telling himself that he wanted only to calm her, and knowing that he lied. She kept her face buried in his shoulder, but her body was melting against his. She was becoming more aroused by the moment and he reveled in the shared sensation of awakening sexual desire.

Mac didn't allow himself to analyze the moment when he abandoned all pretense and allowed his touch to become deliberately erotic. Ariel's instant response electrified him. Her breasts became full and heavy in the palm of his hands, and she lifted her face toward his, her lower body pressing tight against him, her hips undulating in sensuous rhythm. God, she was so wonderfully natural and uninhibited! He was accustomed to lovers who played skillful games to pleasure him and themselves. He wasn't accustomed to partnering a woman whose body reacted with naive, untutored pleasure.

Mac was stunned by the speed and intensity of his own arousal. The knowledge that Ariel wanted him was a more powerful turn-on than the most sophisticated sexual foreplay. He was shattered when she suddenly pulled away from him, wrapping her arms around her waist and turning her head to the side.

"What is it?" he asked softly. "What's wrong, Ariel?"

She spoke disjointedly. "Mac, we shouldn't be doing this. I mean, it isn't smart for us to get...involved. In fact, it would be real stupid of us to get involved." She gave a tight, choked laugh that was almost a sob. "I guess you could say there's no future in it for us."

"Perhaps not, but does that mean we are prohibited from enjoying the pleasures of the moment?" He was surprised at how badly he still wanted to make love to her. Custom dictated that when a woman said no, a man backed off right away.

"Not prohibited," she said. "It just wouldn't be very wise."

"But very, very desirable. Besides, I was not aware that your culture paid so much heed to wisdom." He gave a silent mental groan. Right on, Mac. Insult her, that's a great way to win her over.

"We're individuals, Mac, not a group entity. I'm one of those people who tries to be sensible about my . . . my sexual partners." She gave another little hiccuping breath. "Apart from anything else, we don't have time for this."

"You're right, we don't." He crooked his finger under her chin and tipped her head back a little, so that he could look straight into her eyes. He felt again the shock of intimacy that came from holding someone this close without any form of facial covering to veil their feelings. How odd it was to look into Ariel's face and see all his own confusion, his own uncertain desire reflected there. Delicate pink color rose and faded in her cheeks. Her hazel eyes were stormy and unsettled, sparking with a hint of unmistakable passion. It was disturbing to realize that she could probably read all the same muddled emotions in his own naked face.

God, he wanted to kiss her! Against all the tenets of his upbringing, Mac felt his head dip slowly and inexorably toward her mouth. In his experience, kissing was an act that occurred only after sexual union, with longtime partners who chose to commit the ultimate act of intimacy and unmask their faces. This urge to kiss Ariel before they proceeded beyond the basic preliminaries of physical intimacy was alien to the habits and teachings of a lifetime.

The brush of her unprotected skin against his unshaven cheeks sent an erotic charge racing through his whole body, but she didn't draw back, and he gradually closed the infinitesimal gap between his mouth and hers. When their lips finally touched, the heat and softness of her mouth felt more arousing than any act of sexual foreplay he could possibly have imagined. Dear God, how amazingly erotic it was to kiss a woman who had never been your sexual partner! His body shook with the force of his desire.

For a second or two, he was disoriented by the strangeness of kissing a woman he had known for less than twenty-four hours. Then the heat and passion of her response drowned out every other thought, every other sensation.

She put her arms around his neck and her fingers moved restlessly in the thick strands of his hair. Through the cotton of his T-shirt, he felt her hardened nipples thrust against him. Normally, he would simply have noted this sign of her arousal, and raised their intimacy to a slightly higher level. But coupled with the devastating pressure of her mouth against his, he found this evidence of her desire intoxicating. His control, normally absolute, slipped away.

"Open your mouth," he murmured against her lips, and when she complied, he slid his tongue between her lips, his body shaking with the force of his own desire. He had always taken pride in offering his partners carefully planned and technically skillful sex. It had become something of a good-natured joke among his friends that he could always find some new, exotic and luxurious setting in which to stage his elaborate seductions. In all modesty, he knew that he had acquired a reputation among his women friends as a man who could provide them with unique sexual pleasure.

But with Ariel, his technical knowledge seemed to disappear, burned away by the consuming fire of his own need. He kissed her hungrily, hotly, roughly, with an urgency his own people would have considered close to obscene. She kissed him back with a passion that struck right at the heart of him. If some remnant of civilizing inhibitions hadn't intervened, he would probably have taken her right where they were, on the concrete steps, with both of them sweating and covered in dust, and in imminent danger of being interrupted by anyone who chose to use the stairs.

It was Pip who sounded the first warning, reminding him that Ariel had no birth-control implant and that sex with her was therefore forbidden. Even so, it took all of Mac's training in the most advanced techniques of self-control before he managed to break off their kiss. He released his hold on Ariel abruptly, turning away for a couple of seconds, afraid that if he looked at her, he would want to kiss her again. And if he kissed her again, they would mate. It was inevitable.

So he spoke without looking at her. "I'm sorry," he said gruffly, because he was having trouble catching his breath.

"There's nothing to apologize for." Her voice was almost as husky as his. "What did Pip say?"

"Pip reminded me that you have no birth-control implant."

"Oh, I see. How efficient."

Her voice sounded embarrassed and a little forlorn. Mac finally had himself enough under control to turn around. "You would not have become pregnant, Ariel, even if we had mated, because my own implant is still in place."

"How doubly efficient."

He winced at the sting in her voice. "I am well aware that your sexual customs are different from my own, Ariel, and that you don't view sexual relations in the same light as we do. I'm not sure what I can say, except to apologize for taking advantage of your willingness to be kissed."

"It's our kiss that's bothering you?" The look she gave him, of mingled exasperation and amusement, had become all too familiar over the past several hours. "You kiss very nicely, Mac, and I enjoyed it. Let's not make a big deal out of this, okay? We have more important matters to attend to right now."

"Okay." He spoke the familiar slang word stiffly, frustrated by his inability to make her understand, and even more frustrated by his inability to take their relationship to its natural conclusion. His body, unused to the sensation of unfulfilled lust, felt clumsy and awkward. Not to mention tired and hungry.

"You are correct to remind me that I need to concentrate on finding Consuela," he said, forcing his mind back to business. His body, presumably, would eventually realize that sexual release was not on the agenda and respond accordingly. He sure as hell hoped so.

"I have something that might help us a little," Ariel said, holding out a small plastic card. "When Consuela kicked me, I think this must have fallen out of her pocket."

Mac took the card and looked at the tiny photograph of Consuela, and the name underneath it which wasn't Consuela Timmons, but Frances Foster. "Is it some form of official identification?" he asked.

Ariel nodded. "A driver's license, which you need in order to drive a car. Most adults in the States have one. This one for Consuela is issued by the state of Colorado, although obviously it's a fake."

"We can't assume that. Just because I have never traveled back to your time before, it doesn't mean that this is Consuela's first visit here. Perhaps she learned to drive a car, and applied for her license on a previous trip. And even if it is a fake, I can guarantee that Consuela will have inserted all the records into the necessary computers to make it appear entirely genuine to anyone who checks on it."

"The address on the license is in Edwards, Colorado. I don't know where that is, though. Maybe it's a suburb of Denver? Can you think of any reason why Consuela would be going to Denver?"

Mac shook his head. "No reason at all. But then, I can't imagine why she chose to come back to 1996, so it's not surprising that I can't determine where she would want to go once she got here. I'll ask Pip to locate Edwards for us. At least that will give us a place to start looking."

Pip responded to his question about Edwards with a spectacular holographic image of snow-touched mountain peaks, quivering yellow aspen, winding roads and even a restful sound effect of water rushing over rocks. Pip directed an arrow of red light to Edwards, which turned out to be a small mountain town almost a hundred and fifty miles west of Denver, and about twenty miles west of Vail. Ariel's face lit up like a child's when Pip embellished the map with a pair of foraging deer and a bear, lurking at the entrance to his den.

"Pip really does great maps," she said, smiling.

"Because this Pip was programmed as an entertainment provider," Mac said, wishing he could make her smile like that more often.

"Well, at least we know where Consuela's going. Now all we have to do is work out how we can get ourselves to Colorado without anybody noticing what we're doing."

Ariel sounded so optimistic that Mac didn't have the heart to point out that having a driver's license printed with an address in Edwards didn't mean that Consuela was about to go there. "First, we must find somewhere to rest for a couple of hours while we make our plans," he said. "I programmed Pip to speed up the metabolic processes of your body so that you would be able to heal faster from the blows Consuela inflicted on you. In a very short while, you will find that your body extracts the price of such swift healing. You will experience an overwhelming need to sleep."

"We need to rent ourselves that motel room I keep talking about," Ariel said. "Fortunately, that's no problem now that I know Pip can access the money in my bank account. I saw a bank-teller machine in the hospital's main lobby, and I noticed there's a motel right across the street." She gave a tiny grin. "We won't even need to steal another car."

Mac put his arm around her waist, supporting her. "Then let's go. Bed sounds wonderful to me. Did Consuela inflict further damage on your ankle? Do you need me to carry you?"

"No. In fact, I think Pip's speeded-up healing process must have worked on my ankle, too. It's feeling a lot less painful, so I guess I can walk without your help." She flicked her hair back from her shoulders in a convincing display of unconcern. Mac wasn't deceived. Her ankle might be feeling better, but he knew exactly why she didn't want him to carry her.

They made their way downstairs, then had to lurk in the shadows of the lobby for a few minutes until the banking machine was deserted, but once they had it to themselves, Pip made short work of scanning the simple, electronic controls, and accessing Ariel's account. The automatic teller was programmed to limit withdrawals to two hundred dollars in any twenty-four hour period. Pip wrote an override command and, at Ariel's suggestion, authorized the machine to dispense a thousand dollars.

"This should keep us going for a while," Ariel said. "But we've taken a big risk in withdrawing this money. The police have probably asked the bank to keep a watch on my account, so it won't be long before the authorities know that I somehow managed to overdraw the official bank limit by eight hundred dollars. And they'll know which machine I used, too."

"Naturally, I made sure that Pip obliterated the trail of our activities," Mac said. "According to the records the bank will find, you have withdrawn money from bank-teller machines all across the state of California, ten dollars at a time, in one hundred separate transactions. The police will have no way of knowing that you withdrew money from this machine until somebody physically checks the supply of dollar bills and discovers a thousand dollars missing."

Ariel chuckled, then looked guilty. "I don't know what's the matter with me," she muttered. "Ever since I met you, I've been transforming myself into a career criminal."

"I doubt it," Mac said. "Your conscience works far too much overtime for you to become a successful criminal." He was about to say something more, when Pip gave the soft, low buzz that indicated a law enforcement official had entered scanning range. Putting his arm around Ariel's shoulder, Mac drew her close, and bent down as if nuzzling her neck.

"A single police vehicle has entered the hospital," he said quietly. "Pip says that the officers have been dispatched in response to a citizen's warning that the two of us are roaming the corridors of the hospital." Unable to keep the bitterness out of his voice, he added, "I cannot imagine that we have provoked the interest of ordinary citizens, so Consuela must have been busy. Let's start moving toward the exit."

"We can't, they're here already," Ariel muttered. "Coming in the main entrance now. Two of them, a man and a woman, both in uniform."

"Damn! Put the money into your pocket, very casually, and we shall walk, arm in arm, to the exit. No, don't look toward the police officers. Look up, into my eyes, or look ahead. If you don't act guilty, they will not notice you."

Mac managed to sneak a quick glance at the cops. The woman officer looked as if she'd been around long enough to know what she was doing; the man looked fresh out of police academy. Both of them, unfortunately, seemed to be scrutinizing the people in the lobby with close attention. Mac shuffled to the exit, resisting the urge to swing Ariel up into his arms and run like hell.

They might have made it outside successfully unobserved except for the fact that Pip suddenly let out a high-pitched squawk of alarm and announced in loud Spanglish that a second squad car was entering the hospital parking lot.

The officers already inside the hospital swung around, searching for the source of the screech. The minute they saw Mac and Ariel, he knew it was all over. The female cop broke into a run, heading across the lobby at full speed. The young rookie looked bewildered, then followed suit.

Mac had about two seconds to come up with an escape plan, and he did the best he could. He gave Pip a frantic command, and a huge holographic pitbull, drool slathering from its jaws, materialized in the center of the lobby, right in front of the police officers. They skidded to a halt, yelling to bystanders to stay back.

Mac didn't hang around to find out how long it would take them to realize the dog had no bite to back up its alarming bark. He swung Ariel up into his arms, and dashed for their abandoned Saturn.

"Get us out of here," he panted, shoving her behind the wheel, jumping into the passenger seat and giving Pip the order to turn on the ignition, almost in one motion.

She backed out of the parking space. "Mac, we can't go on like this. We've got to stop running."

"Agreed. But not right this minute, okay?"

She swung the car in a wide circle and looped back to the exit gate. She looked at him, her mouth taut and her eyes dark with panic. "Where shall I go now? We have maybe ten miles of gas left, tops."

"Get back on the highway. We will exit at the first motel we see."

Ariel drove onto the access ramp. "That'll be the first place the police check."

He shook his head. "No, why should they? It would be far more natural to assume that we're driving as far away as we can."

"This car has probably been reported stolen by now. The police will be looking for it, as well as for us."

"Then we must make sure that when we stop, this car is not visible from the road. We'll have to find another car when we want to move on."

"I'm not stealing any more cars," Ariel said.

He smiled wryly. "I wonder why I am not surprised? How inconvenient that you are such a very law-abiding citizen, Ariel."

"Law-abiding!" Her words fizzed with pent-up frustration. "If there are any laws I haven't broken in the past twenty-four hours, it's purely by coincidence!"

He laughed, and realized with astonishment just how infrequently he'd laughed when he was in Consuela's company.

"I see nothing in the least amusing about our situation," she said primly.

Whenever she pursed her lips in that stubborn, uncompromising pout, he developed the strongest urge to kiss her. He quickly redirected his thoughts into more appropriate channels. "Take this exit," he said. "Look, there's a motel just off the highway."

"Good grief! Roach haven," she muttered, nevertheless directing the Saturn onto the ramp. The car sputtered and she pounded the steering wheel, alternately murmuring curses and endearments. She turned into the parking lot of the motel, and the car engine made an ominous sputtering sound.

"What is it?" Mac asked. "What's happened?"

She adjusted the gear lever and let the car roll down an incline toward a distant corner of the lot. "We just ran out of gas," she said. "I guess this is where we're going to be staying for a while."

"If they have beds, I love it already."

"Wait till you see inside the rooms. The Rolling Stones Motel. Real cute. I'm betting this place hasn't seen a lick of paint on its doors since 1970. What do you think?"

Mac grinned, pleased that he would be able to make this experience much more enjoyable for her than she could imagine. "I have no idea when they last painted the motel, but it doesn't matter. I think you are going to love this place."

"Sure I am. I'm really into pink aluminum siding and tubs of dead geraniums." She got out of the car and slammed the door.

"Trust me," Mac said. "You will be delighted with the interior decor."

She pushed open the door marked Office. A smell of stale cigarette smoke wafted toward them. She coughed. "Right, I can visualize it already. Early Salvation Army."

"I believe not," Mac said, and smiled.

7

AS FAR AS Ariel was concerned, the motel had one major attribute in its favor: the clerk who registered them wasn't even slightly interested in asking questions. When Ariel said she would be paying cash, up front, he charged them sixty-five dollars, fifteen more than the amount stated on the coffee-stained rate card, and seemed to consider that this entitled them not only to a room at the rear of the motel, but also to a complete absence of curiosity about where they'd come from and why they had no luggage.

Ariel was delighted to have avoided the expected difficulties at check-in time, but her optimism was severely dented when they reached their room. The decor was everything she'd feared, with beige walls yellowed by the smoke of thousands of cigarettes, a mustard-brown shag carpet that undoubtedly provided home for a marching brigade of bugs with overbites and shabby bedspreads hung drunkenly over mattresses that visibly sagged toward the middle.

The only consolation was that the bathroom seemed slightly less dilapidated than the bedroom, and the sheets on the sagging beds were not only clean, but relatively new. In her state of near exhaustion, Ariel was prepared to put up with a lot for the sake of a nap on freshly laundered sheets.

Mac stepped gingerly around the stained Formica-topped table shoved next to the grimy window. "This is not very hygienic," he said poking one of the beds as if he expected it to bite him. Not an altogether unreasonable fear, Ariel decided wryly.

"It won't be so bad once we take off these ratty bedspreads." She tried to sound cheerful. "Actually, the sheets are surprisingly clean—"

"I would hate to enter a room you considered surprisingly dirty," Mac said gloomily.

"Look on the bright side," Ariel said. "There's a bar of new soap and a bottle of cheap shampoo in the bathroom, so we'll be able to take showers after we nap. We may be fugitives from the law, but by golly, we're going to be well-scrubbed fugitives."

Mac straightened from his inspection of the beds and smiled at her. "You are a remarkable woman, Ariel Hutton, did you know that?" He rid the beds of their hideous maroon spreads, wincing at the sight of multiple cigarette burns in the blankets. He quickly turned the covers back to expose clean white sheets and sat down with a sigh of relief. "First things first," he said. "Food. How do we order food?"

"We can check the phone book to find out which nearby restaurants deliver," Ariel said. "Do you eat pizza? There's bound to be a pizza place not too far away."

"I don't know what pizza is, but as long as it contains no meat or fish products, I'm eager to give it a try."

Ariel reached for the Yellow Pages. "Are you a vegetarian, Mac?"

"Everyone in my world is a vegetarian. In fact, most of what we eat is artificially synthesized from soy protein and cellulose, although we do eat freshly grown fruit and vegetables as flavor enhancers on special occasions."

"If most things are artificially synthesized, do you have chefs and gourmet cooks?" Ariel asked, flipping through the listings for takeout food. "Or do you buy your food in packages, ready to eat?"

"A little of both. My parents, in fact, owned a small restaurant, but I don't have much time to cook, so I buy my meals ready-prepared."

Ariel scribbled down the number of a restaurant that promised made-to-order pizzas with twenty-minute delivery. Mac appeared a little embarrassed when he reached out to stop her dialing. "If it is okay with you, Ariel, I would be most grateful if you would not order a dish that contains meat for yourself. I know that humans ate meat and fish for thousands of years, but such practices have been forbidden for over a century, and I would find it difficult to watch you eating the dead flesh of an animal bred only to be slaughtered."

Dead flesh? Ariel shuddered. Described in such terms, the pepperoni sausage she'd been looking forward to sounded considerably less appealing. "We'll order mushrooms and double cheese for both of us," she said, dialing the restaurant. "You don't mind eating dairy products, do you?"

"I love cheese," he said. "Although I don't believe I've ever actually eaten any that was made with real milk." He yawned and lay back against the pillows. "We're so short of space in my world, that we can't afford to have cows occupying land that could be used to house people. I love eggs, too. I eat real ones each year on my birthday and to hell with the expense."

It was difficult to think of an egg as a major birthday treat. A voice came on the line to take her order before Ariel could reply. She gave their room number at the motel and requested a large pizza and a six-pack of cola. Since Mac wasn't likely to be around for much longer, she figured that he ought to at least taste the staples of the late-twentieth-century diet. Then she sat cross-legged on the bed, determined to pretend for the next few minutes that Consuela didn't exist, and that she and Mac could afford the luxury of chatting casually, and learning about each other's cultures.

"Tell me more about your world," she said. "Do children still go to school? Do men and women still get married? Do people have jobs, or do computers and machines take care of all the work?"

He smiled and ticked off the answers on his fingers. "Children still go to school. In fact, most people remain students until they are almost thirty because we consider education so important. No, we don't get married, at least not in the way you understand the word. And yes, machines and computers do much of the work in our world, but of course most people still have jobs."

"What sorts of jobs?"

"Well, someone has to design the machines and the computers that clean the streets, and manufacture our household goods. Machines synthesize our food, it is true, but we need chefs and nutritionists to experiment with ways to make the ingredients healthier and tastier. And however great our technology becomes, we still need artists and musicians, athletes and astronauts, politicians and archaeologists, not to mention police officers and doctors and teachers and research scientists and philosophers."

"It all sounds surprisingly normal," Ariel said. "Except it's difficult for me to imagine a world in which people set off to work each day, stark naked, unless you count a layer of multihued body paint as clothes."

"Nakedness is in the mind," Mac said. "I have discovered that for myself since I arrived here in your time. For you, nakedness means an absence of cloth draped over certain parts of the body. For me, nakedness means an absence of permapel masking the face."

She touched her cheeks, which suddenly felt hot, and realized that Mac usually avoided looking directly into her face. But whenever he did, she felt an immediate charge of sexual awareness. It was an odd feeling to know that as far as Mac was concerned, she was walking around in a state of major undress.

"You said that you don't have marriages as we understand them," she said, changing the subject to one that didn't leave her so acutely aware of Mac's presence on the bed next to her. "So what exactly was this Silver Ceremony you and Consuela were celebrating when she killed her sis—" Ariel broke off in midsentence, annoyed with herself for introducing Consuela's name into their conversation. Still, since the deed was done, she decided she might as well finish her question. "Didn't you and Consuela have to get married before the government approved your application to become parents?"

Mac shook his head. "We have split up the concepts of marriage and parenthood," he said. "During the Great Famine, it became obvious that not only were we human beings reproducing ourselves to the point of extinction, we were also squandering the lives of the children we gave birth to with careless abandon. The level of violence had reached the point that murder was the number-one cause of death. And this at a time when famine was wiping out thousands of our citizens each day. Sociologists and psychologists and government officials, not to mention our religious leaders, all launched massive campaigns to persuade people to take marriage and parenthood more seriously, but the campaigns failed. Eighty percent of marriages ended in divorce, and two-thirds of all children grew up with only a single parent to care for them. At a certain point, we decided the institution of marriage was meaningless in terms of the way people actually behaved, so the government abolished marriage as a legal concept at the end of the twenty-first century."

"And the churches agreed to the abolition of something so integral to the fabric of human society?" Ariel asked, scarcely believing what she was hearing.

"Religious leaders still married people, but the ceremony had no status in law. Eventually, a famous sociologist called LaVera Travis came up with the brilliant insight that people get married because they are sexually attracted to each other, but the qualities that make for good parents have almost nothing to do with sexual attraction."

"I'm not sure that's a brilliant insight," Ariel protested. "I've read dozens of articles that make much the same point."

"Yes, but LaVera Travis's great contribution to the debate was that she came up with a practical solution to our double problem of overpopulation and unstable marriages. LaVera managed to convince people that, in an era in which we had methods of birth control that were a hundred percent safe and effective, there was no reason to link sexual activity to marriage and parenthood."

"I think that's an idea we tried out in the 1960s," Ariel said dryly, thinking of her parents and their flirtation with the concepts of communal living and free love. "We called it the sexual revolution and we found that it had significant drawbacks."

"Perhaps because you took the revolution only halfway," Mac suggested. "If you think about it, the reason society needs couples to stay together is so that they'll form a solid family unit for their children, not because they're sexually active. LaVera Travis understood this and suggested our country needed a new morality. Everyone in my world is implanted with a permanent birth-control device the day they're born. After that, we're free to form any sort of sexual liaison or partnership we choose, but we're taught from early childhood that having children is a special privilege with a lot of responsibilities. People who want to become parents must take many courses, pass an exam in child care and apply for a government license. They must also agree to live together for a minimum period of twenty years, so that they provide a home for their child at least until he or she has finished high school."

"But what happens if the parents discover that they can't bear to live together?" Ariel asked.

"Then we have something which is similar to your concept of divorce," Mac said. "But you'd be surprised how rarely parents choose to break their vows. Remember, Silver Partners have only sworn to be dedicated parents, they haven't promised to be lifelong monogamous sexual partners. Right there, the new morality has taken away one of the great pressures that destroyed so many marriages."

In Ariel's opinion, the new morality also seemed to have taken away a good part of the special bond that made the difference between loving families and efficient foster care. On the other hand, she had to admit that for the millions of children growing up in broken homes, or with neglectful and violent parents, the idea of having two adults devoted exclusively to your well-being would seem like heaven. "How do prospective parents find each other? Or does the government make that choice for you, too?"

"Of course not. We are a democracy not a totalitarian state. We find our partners in all the same ways that you meet your prospective mates. Usually, people who plan to become Silver Partners live together for several months to be sure they're compatible."

"How did you meet Consuela?" Ariel asked.

He grimaced. "President Timmons introduced us at a party. We were instantly attracted to each other, and delighted when we discovered that we both had parenting licenses, and that we both wanted to have a daughter." He corrected himself, voice taut. "Or perhaps I should say that I was instantly attracted and Consuela was relieved to have found precisely the sucker she needed to pursue her political plans."

Ariel put her hand over his. "Self-pity, Mac?"

"Yes, damn you. A strong attack." He smiled at her with no more than a hint of strain. "No wonder we all wear face masks in my time. It's a lot easier to appear noble and intelligent when every twitch of a muscle doesn't reveal what you're really feeling."

She reached up and brushed her fingers lightly across his high cheekbones. "Maybe, but it's easier to make friends when you can tell what people are thinking."

He caught her hands and looked down at her, eyes dark. "I do not doubt it," he said huskily. "And I think we are becoming friends, no?"

"Yes," she said, her heart beating a little faster. "I guess we are."

"I thank you for acting as my friend, Ariel."

"You're welcome. I'm really glad that we met." Ariel left her hands within his clasp, aware of a lump of regret forming in her throat when she thought of Mac's inevitable departure. "Tell me more about your world," she said, trying to sound cheerful. "What happens when a couple gets together and decides they want to become parents? Who removes the birth-control implant? Who decides how many children the couple can have?"

"Once they've completed all the legal agreements, the friends and family of the prospective parents arrange a special ceremony. The couple declares in front of the assembled witnesses that they have agreed to become Silver Partners. They announce the sex of the child they've chosen to bear, and a family member opens the sealed license to show whether the partners will be permitted one child or, in some cases, two children, so that our society doesn't completely lose the experience of growing up with brothers and sisters. The number of children you can have is decided by lottery, so that it will be as fair as possible...."

Ariel was appalled now that she finally realized the full significance of the moment Consuela had chosen to murder her sister. "How could Consuela have utilized such a special occasion to kill her sister?" she asked, feeling a burst of pain and anger on Mac's behalf.

"Because it was the only way to achieve her objective," he said, his voice harsh. "Naturally, the president is guarded at all times, but the level of security I'd ordered was at its lowest point because of the intimate nature of the new-parent ceremony, and the fact that President Timmons and I knew every guest personally. The president had just unsealed our license and read that it permitted us to have a single child, when Consuela murdered her. She deliberately chose the most solemn moment to kill her sister, seconds before our birth-control implants would have been removed and the bond between us would have become irrevocable."

His mouth tightened and he turned his head, staring out of the dirty window, although Ariel doubted if he saw much of the view. "We had spent so many hours planning for the birth of our daughter," he said, his voice filled with regret. "We had chosen Liliana for her name, argued about the school she would attend, marveled over the wonderful baby gifts our friends had sent us, planned the inn we would visit on the night of her conception."

"Oh, Mac, I'm so sorry."

"The hell of it is, much as I'd like to blame Consuela for the president's death, the blame really belongs to me. I was so caught up in what a great father I was going to be that I totally let down my guard. If I'd ordered an adequate weapons scan before the ceremony, Consuela wouldn't have been able to get within fifty meters of the president with the firepower she was carrying concealed in her ceremonial belt."

"Don't pile guilt on yourself that you don't deserve," Ariel said. "How could you possibly suspect that Consuela was planning to murder her own sister? There was no way you could have known—"

"It was my job to know," Mac said tersely.

"Don't demand the impossible of yourself," Ariel said, putting her arms around him without stopping to question her need to offer comfort. "Even the nation's top cop doesn't expect treachery from the people he loves."

Mac's body remained stiff in her arms. "There were clues available to me if I'd chosen to see them. I ignored them. I wanted to see only that a beautiful, intelligent and successful woman had agreed to bear my child."

"Why would you expect yourself to see more? You're a regular human being, after all, even if your doctors have learned to pump vitamins into fetuses and make people who can jump like gazelles and run like jaguars. You made a mistake, Mac. We all do that."

"You are right. Unfortunately, some screwups cost more than others. Mine cost our nation its most popular president in fifty years."

"You'll find Consuela and take her back to stand trial. That will go a long way toward healing the wounds, Mac."

"I shall certainly find Consuela or die in the attempt. I owe my country at least that much."

"Of course we'll find her. And when you go back to your own time, you'll find another woman who wants to have a baby daughter as much as you."

Mac shrugged with an indifference that didn't deceive Ariel for a moment. "My parenting license has expired and the government is unlikely to renew it."

"Whyever not?" Ariel exclaimed. "You passed their exams and qualified as a father, didn't you? It's not your fault that Consuela turned out to be a criminal!"

Mac smiled tightly. "Our government is less sentimental than you, Ariel. The world needs to reduce the population if we're to ease the level of misery that still exists despite our best efforts. Less than half the people in our country are allowed the supreme privilege of raising a child, and people who make mistakes the first time around are not usually afforded the luxury of a second chance."

The system Mac described seemed unbearably regimented and intrusive. Ariel's heart contracted as she visualized what it would be like to long for a baby and to be denied that joy by virtue of a government policy. "I can't believe people have changed so much in two hundred years that they accept all these rules and regulations about their private lives without protest. Honestly, Mac, I'm surprised you don't have riots in the streets."

"We don't have riots," Mac said grimly. "But over the last decade, there's been a lot of civil unrest. Consuela claimed to act on behalf of all the citizens deprived of their God-given right to have children. She seemed indifferent to the fact that President Timmons has campaigned tirelessly to increase the percentage of citizens entitled to become parents."

There was nothing that could justify Consuela's brutal act, in Ariel's eyes, but she could understand how people denied the possibility of parenthood could become angry and frustrated enough to take the law into their own hands.

"Consuela was terribly wrong to murder the president," she said. "And especially horrible since the president was her own sister. But Mac, there's plenty of blame to spread around. It's wrong of your government to deny people the right to have a baby. A policy like that is almost begging for violent opposition."

"Is it?" he asked, his voice unusually savage. "In my world, we have a choice between controlling our population by repeated cycles of mass starvation, or controlling it by limiting the number of children born. Which would you prefer?"

"Well, obviously not mass starvation," Ariel said. "But are you sure that there aren't other choices?"

"What other choices do you suggest?"

"Increase food production, maybe. More careful use of resources. Space exploration, if you have the technology—"

"Do you think we haven't struggled to establish colonies on the moon and Mars? Have you any idea how much it costs to sustain an artificial ecosystem in a place that has neither air nor water? As for increasing food production, every square centimeter of land is utilized. Do you know that until I came back to your time, I had never seen a house with a garden, or walked on grass that wasn't growing in a recreational reservation? The problem is not my world's lack of ingenuity. The problem is that your world needed to take decisive action years before anyone in my time was born. Now we're left to pay the price because our ancestors, with their reckless policies, refused to prevent—"

"Wait a minute! What reckless policies? We don't have an official population-control policy—"

"Exactly! Do you know how many families there were in the twenty-first century who were still having eight, or ten, or fifteen children? Do you realize that if ten children each have five children and each of those five children has five more, then in three generations we've gone from one couple, to two hundred and fifty new human beings?"

"I'd never made that calculation," Ariel muttered. "Besides, very few people in the States have more than three children, and most couples only have two, so it's an irrelevant statistic for this country."

"True, so in three generations, the American population merely doubles. That's still quite a problem. Besides, the United States isn't the world, and the planet can only accommodate a certain number of people, whether they happen to have been born in Brooklyn, or Buenos Aires, or Beijing. My country has done the best we could in the situation of horrible overcrowding that we inherited. Our system for selecting parents is completely fair and democratic, which is more than can be said for the systems they've adopted in the Empire of East Asia, or the European Union. In America, anyone can apply for a parenting license, and there is no amount of money or position or influence that can buy you a license you haven't earned. The Americans who become parents are the ones our society judges most likely to be successful in raising a child."

"So the people who fail their parenting tests, the people who aren't allowed to have babies, are supposed to smile and accept that it's all for the greater good of society?"

Mac shook his head. "No, we don't expect them to smile, but we do the best we can with grief counseling and other support systems to help them accept the inevitable. Besides, I think you might be surprised to discover just how many people don't want to have children. We've found over the last fifty years that anywhere from a quarter to a third of our citizens express no interest whatsoever in having babies."

"That leaves between a quarter and a third of your citizens who are desperately unhappy."

"Yes, I know. And Manuela Timmons's political party was gaining power every election, campaigning on the need to increase the number of people who are allowed to have babies, even though it would mean turning some of our national parks into housing developments, and lowering the ration of nonessential food items citizens are allowed to purchase. Personally, I think the trade-off is worth it. I'm also optimistic enough to believe that with our developing technology, Mars Colony will eventually become self-sustaining and help to solve some of our problems. Manuela Timmons was the first person elected to the presidency who'd campaigned on a platform of increased birth licenses. The legislation she proposed failed in Congress, but it would have been reintroduced next session. Consuela's mistake wasn't in feeling sorry for our people who are forbidden to have the children they long for. Her mistake was in trying to kill her way into power."

"If she was trying to seize control of the government, running back to 1996 doesn't seem a very smart way to achieve her goal," Ariel said. "I can't begin to imagine what she hopes to achieve here. And what did she expect to happen after she killed her sister? What was the point of the assassination, if she isn't even there to take advantage of what she's done?"

"She had conspirators in place all over the country, waiting to seize key offices. What she didn't know was that my investigators had infiltrated the conspiracy and were ready to move in and arrest the ringleaders at the first sign of trouble. What I didn't know was that Consuela was the conspiracy's chief ringleader and that she'd planned all along to use our Silver Ceremony as the signal for her fellow conspirators to act." Mac smiled bitterly. "I guess you could say that we both knew only one half of the story, so both of our plans failed."

"But did Consuela fail?" Ariel asked. "Maybe she planned all along to escape back into 1996."

"I think she did. What she didn't expect was that I would follow her. She is—was—the director in chief of time-travel research, and I believe she expected to be able to lock down the time-travel chamber before I reached it."

Ariel was so caught up in their conversation that it took her a moment or two to register the fact that somebody was knocking at the door. "That'll be the pizza," she said. "Maybe you'd better keep out of sight, Mac, just to be on the safe side."

"Okay." Mac slipped into the bathroom and Ariel greeted the delivery boy with what she hoped was just enough

friendliness to ensure that he would have no reason to remember her.

"Thanks," she said, taking the box. "You can put the cola
on the table there. How much do I owe you?"

"Fourteen-fifty." The boy shoved his hands into the pockets of his baggy jeans and snapped his gum. To Ariel's relief,
he looked so bored, she doubted he would have noticed if
she'd sprouted fangs and a tail. She paid him with a twenty
and asked for three dollars back, which seemed the right
amount of tip to pass unnoticed.

"Thanks." The delivery boy ambled to the door, pocket-
ing the change. Some remnant of corporate training seemed
to kick in and he paused in the doorway. "Thanks for calling
Trentino's. Have a nice day."

"Sure. You, too." Ariel closed the door and breathed in the
satisfying smell of melted cheese and spicy tomato sauce. Her
stomach rumbled in happy anticipation. For a moment, she
was more than willing to forget about Consuela and all her
works.

"You can come out, Mac," she called. "We have hot food
and cold drinks. Paradise is at hand."

Mac emerged from the bathroom just as she opened the
box to reveal the bubbling, golden-brown topping on the
pizza. He sniffed deeply and his eyes glazed over. "That is
pizza?" he asked. "That giant portion is just for the two of
us?"

"We don't have to eat it all," Ariel said, ashamed of being
so wasteful when she remembered what Mac had said about
the shortage of food in his time. Still, refusing to eat her share
of the pizza today wasn't going to make a blind bit of difference to the people living in 2196, so she unfolded a paper
napkin and handed Mac a large slice.

"Tell me what you think of real cheese," she said. "The
topping's a mixture of mozzarella and cheddar, with a dash

of parmesan. And inside this can is cola, which is more or less our national drink."

"I know what cola is," he said, taking the can and the slice of pizza. He eyed the food somewhat warily. "The first time a man eats real cheese ought to count as a special occasion, don't you think?"

"Definitely," Ariel said, smiling. "I could hum a few bars of triumphal music if that would help."

"I have a better idea," Mac said, looking pleased with himself. "I think we ought to fix up our surroundings so that they look a bit more festive. Would you like that?"

"I'd love it. Unfortunately, I don't know how we do it. It's a bit late to send out for flowers, and anyway, we need to save our money."

"For once, I have all the answers." Mac took off his Pip and swung it by its silver chain. "You remember that I told you this was a gift from President Timmons? She planned for Consuela and me to take it on our conception trip, so it isn't very efficient either as an information provider, or as a law enforcement device. But she had it programmed to be the last word in entertainment luxury. Tell me your fantasy setting, and Pip can probably provide it."

"I don't think I understand."

"Pip can create fifteen thousand different scenes for our viewing pleasure. Would you like to eat in a forest? By the ocean? In a rocket heading for the moon? This Pip is programmed to provide the setting of your choice. That's what I meant when I said you would love the decor of this room."

"Wow! You mean Pip can create a sort of giant picture window?" Ariel eyed the tiny pulsing tube with new respect. "But will it work without all sorts of fancy gadgets to hook into?"

"Pip is entirely self-contained," Mac said. "Tell me your idea of the perfect place for us to eat pizza together."

"A street café in Florence," Ariel said promptly, although she couldn't imagine how a computer, however powerful, could transform a tacky California motel room into a Florentine café. "It would be great if Pip could give us a view of an Italian piazza, with a fountain in the center of the square, a tenor singing love songs in the background and the sun just setting overhead."

Mac bowed with a mock flourish. "Your wish is my command, *signorina*. I hope." He gave a string of instructions to Pip, who rumbled back brief responses. For twenty seconds or so, nothing happened. Then gradually, the shabby room filled with the sounds of a lilting rendition of "O Sole Mio," the sound quality so perfect that Ariel jerked her head around, looking for the singer, even though she knew that Pip must have activated some sort of recording device.

The music faded into the distance. Then, before her disbelieving gaze, the shabby walls of their room disappeared, to be replaced by a view of a piazza so real that for a moment or two she felt physically disoriented by the abrupt transformation, as if she'd been snatched out of the motel room by a giant hand and set down in a country town in Tuscany with no time to catch her breath. Pip, she realized, hadn't provided just a picture window, but a three-dimensional scene.

As she gazed around, trying to absorb the full, realistic splendor of the piazza, an elderly woman strolled into view and stopped at the flower stall directly opposite them. She bought a bouquet of yellow jonquils, tucked them into her basket and strolled off, humming. The tenor began to sing again, and Ariel finally spotted him high up behind the open casement windows of a balcony.

A pair of giggling boys ran to the center of the square and splashed each other with water that gurgled out of the stone mouths of fishes poised in eternal frolic on the lip of the fountain. A young man on a motor scooter shot past, so close that Ariel felt the heat of his engine exhaust on her skin. If she hadn't still been clutching the back of the rickety motel chair, Ariel would have staked her life on the fact that they were sitting in a café at the corner of an Italian piazza, watching local life unfold.

"How can Pip do this?" she asked Mac when she finally managed to speak. "How can a computer that tiny create such a powerful illusion? What's happened to the walls of our room? How can Pip bring an entire public square into a bedroom that can't be bigger than fifteen by twenty feet?"

"Pip is merely projecting a holographic image, and adding some sounds and smells to make the image more realistic," Mac said, and as he spoke the sound of singing lowered just slightly so that he didn't need to raise his voice in order to be heard. "Give me your hand, and you'll see that if you try to touch any of these objects, there's nothing there. See? No water, no flowers, no café with cheerful red tablecloths. The illusion of distance and perspective is just that, an illusion. This scene is merely an extension of the same holographic technology that Pip used to provide maps for us, and to create the image of a vicious dog that barred the path of the cops who were chasing us at the hospital."

Feeling like a child presented with a fabulous new toy, Ariel gave a twirl of sheer pleasure before sitting on the rickety metal chair, which now appeared to stand not on brown shag carpet, but on the flagstoned sidewalk surrounding the cobbled piazza. The window with its drooping vertical blinds, looking onto the concrete parking lot, had given way to a view of the sun, slowly dipping behind distant hills, and the two sagging beds had disappeared behind the illusory wall of an old-fashioned grocery store, hung with pasta and strings of onions.

The scene was so perfect that Ariel felt precariously poised between tears and laughter. She cleared her throat a couple of times and popped the top on a can of soda. "Here," she said, handing it to Mac. "We need a jug of Chianti to be really in keeping with our surroundings, but you'll find iced cola goes down well with the pizza."

"Thanks." Mac took a long swallow, then turned to watch as a little girl, scarcely more than a toddler, skipped down the road holding her mother's hand, her braids bouncing on her chubby shoulders. She smiled and waved as she passed their table.

Ariel laughed and waved back. "Gosh, I can't believe she was just a moving picture. Mac, thank you. This is wonderful. I honest-to-goodness feel as if I'm in Italy. I hope you're not too bored by it all."

"I'm not bored at all. Italy has always been one of my favorite places to visit. I'm particularly fond of Florence during the Renaissance, although I always instruct Pip to go easy on the smells and the scenes of public flogging."

Ariel shook her head, trying to get used to the idea that Pip could probably transform their motel room into a perfect replica of the Roman Forum if Mac gave it the appropriate command. The toys for people in the twenty-second century were certainly lots of fun, she decided, although they didn't make up for the luxury of having a house with a garden, and the freedom to marry and have children.

She pushed the paper plate with its slice of mushroom pizza across to Mac. "Eat this while it's still warm," she said. "We seem to have gotten lucky with our choice of restaurant—it's pretty good pizza. Great crust."

Mac examined the pizza for several seconds before finally taking a bite and chewing carefully, his face so devoid of expression that Ariel got worried. She'd been hoping Mac would enjoy eating real food.

"Mac, if you don't like it, I'm sure we could find a restaurant willing to deliver something more basic. You don't have to be polite about the pizza. I guess I'd be pretty unhappy if I traveled back to colonial America and discovered they expected me to eat minced squirrel or something."

He didn't answer with words, just shook his head and took another bite. His mouth gradually relaxed into a huge smile, and his eyes gleamed with mingled astonishment and pleasure. "It is wonderful," he said. "The most delicious food I have ever eaten."

"You like it!" Ariel smiled in delight.

"Like it? It's out of this world." He licked a string of melted mozzarella from his fingers and grimaced ruefully. "I always used to like syncheez. Now I believe I will never be able to eat it again without remembering how the real thing tastes."

The sun sank lower behind the hills as they talked and ate, turning the sky pink and flooding the room with the soft purple shadows of evening. The tenor stopped singing, but far away in the distance, a church bell rang out, and the crystal-pure sounds of a Gregorian chant drifted into the square.

They ate their way through three-quarters of the pizza while Mac asked her endless questions about her family, and what it felt like to live in a world where empty space still abounded. Ariel told him about her sister, and Miranda's success as an actress, and made him laugh as she described her unconventional parents and the amazing summers she'd spent camping out in the wilderness, or growing organic food at a communal farm in Michigan, or the memorable year when her parents had decided to raft down the Amazon, searching the rain forest for medicinal plants, with Miranda and Ariel in tow.

"You are very lucky," Mac said, leaning back in his chair and reluctantly refusing her offer of another slice of pizza. "I can tell just from listening to you how much you love and admire your parents. And your sister, too, of course."

Ariel stared at him in shocked silence. Was it true? she wondered. Had Mac, listening to her with an outsider's ears, detected the truth that she'd never been willing to acknowledge? That she admired her parents for having had the courage to live out their outlandish convictions, and for including her and Miranda in the ongoing adventure that they'd made of their lives? It was a startling insight, and one she would have to consider later, when there was more time.

The Gregorian chant faded into silence. The shadows lengthened. A white-aproned shopkeeper emerged from the little grocery store and took in his strings of onions and packets of homemade pasta.

"Time for us to rest." Mac stood up, pulling Ariel with him. He held her for a moment within the circle of his arms. "I will program Pip to wake us in one hour," he said. "By then, it will be starting to get dark outside and we can decide our next move. But now, I believe we both need to sleep more than we need to plan. This has been a rough twenty-four hours for both of us."

Ariel felt so drowsy that she was having trouble keeping her eyes open. "I don't understand why I feel so sleepy all of a sudden," she said.

"Pip is altering your brain waves into a pattern that induces sleep." Mac spoke a few words in Spanglish and the Italian market square gradually disappeared into total darkness. Natural light returned, revealing only their own motel room with the ugly walls and sagging beds.

Ariel spared a moment of regret for the lost piazza, but her desire for sleep was so overwhelming that the bed looked even more inviting than the fountain and flower stall. She kicked off her shoes, and flopped onto the mattress, her head falling onto the pillow almost of its own volition.

"Sleep well," Mac said softly.

She was asleep before she could answer.

8

ARIEL WOKE to the sound of wind chimes, and the caress of a soft breeze that carried within it the perfume of spring flowers. Still drowsy with sleep, she rolled over in bed and came into contact with a length of hard, muscled and definitely masculine thigh.

Mac. She knew at once where she was and who was lying in bed with her, but she felt no urge to move away, or to protest the intimacy of their position. So much for the king-size bed in her town house, bought so that she would never have to touch her lover while she slept. As if she could possibly make love with a man she didn't want to sleep close to! Ariel rubbed her eyes, stretching sleepily, feeling her skin rub intimately against Mac's.

He put his hand on her hip, the gesture at once possessive and oddly reassuring. "Welcome back," he said, and his smile gleamed momentarily white in the shadowed twilight of their room.

She propped her chin on her hand, resting on her elbow. Mac was very close, but now that she was fully awake, he moved away until there was a six-inch gap between their bodies. She found herself wishing that he wouldn't be quite so considerate.

"Did I oversleep?" she asked.

"Only by ten minutes."

She yawned and stretched. "I feel almost like a normal human being again. Even my ankle's stopped hurting."

"I had Pip work on it some more, but it's not healed completely."

The wind chimes tinkled a mellow, broken scale through the open window at her back and she turned slightly, catching a glimpse of a magnolia tree in full bloom. Pip—and Mac—had obviously been busy while she slept. Intrigued by her new virtual surroundings, she sat up in bed, looking around the elegant, but subtly alien room that Pip had superimposed over the dreary decor of the motel.

"Where are we?" she asked. "What is this place?"

Mac understood that she wasn't asking about their physical location in the motel. "I asked Pip to reproduce the living room of my housing unit," he said. "I enjoyed seeing your home very much and I thought you might like to see mine."

"Oh yes, that was a wonderful idea, Mac, thank you." She leaned forward, drinking in the details of the sparsely furnished room. The aura was vaguely Japanese in its simplicity, an impression that was emphasized by the absence of chairs and the piles of giant, silk-covered cushions scattered around two low tables of lacquered wood. In the far corner of the room, three interwoven tubes of glass gave out an ever-changing flicker of colored light, and the ceiling displayed a panorama of clouds chugging across a rain-swept spring sky. The walls weren't painted, or papered, but seemed to be made out of a substance that glowed with a faint silvery luminescence, somehow adding to the impression of coolness and absence of clutter. There were no shelves, no knickknacks, and no rugs on the gleaming tiled floor, but a touch of domesticity was provided by a square screen set into the wall, which displayed a series of pictures—almost like snapshots—each one remaining in the frame for twenty seconds or so before a new one flashed into view.

"Are those pictures of your family?" Ariel asked.

He nodded. "That's my mother," he said, ordering Pip to freeze on a frame of a handsome woman with high cheekbones and straight, raven-black hair, holding a very young baby, almost invisible beneath the blanket swaddling him.

"Are you the baby?" she asked, oddly touched to see that where newborn infants were concerned, permapel hadn't replaced fluffy cotton, even two hundred years into the future.

He nodded. "And this is my father," he said as the picture of a ruddy-cheeked, sandy-haired man flashed onto the screen.

"You look much more like your mother," Ariel said.

He grinned. "Well, I have my father's eyes and, according to Mom, a double dose of his obstinacy to make up for the fact that my bone structure and coloring are hers."

"Are they both still alive?"

"Very much so. They're only in their seventies and most people in my time can look forward to celebrating their hundredth birthday."

Ariel turned around on the bed so that she could look out of the room's only window. Outside, a garden bloomed with all the vivid freshness of early spring, the entrance gate shaded by the blossoming magnolia tree she'd glimpsed on waking, a mist of fine rain drizzling out of a sky that matched the interior ceiling.

"Do you take care of the garden yourself?" she asked. "If so, you must have green fingers and toes, not just green thumbs."

"I wish I could claim credit," Mac said. "But the garden isn't real, it's a videoscape. I've set the scene to grow and wither with the seasons, and I can tinker with the program to choose what flowers and shrubs I want to plant, and how often the grass is going to get cut, all that sort of thing, but that's as close to reality as my garden gets."

Ariel felt so sorry for him that she didn't know what to say. She wondered if he was allowed real live houseplants, or whether he'd have to apply for a government license for those, too. "How interesting," she managed to say at last. "Does your apartment have any windows with real views?"

He shook his head. "It doesn't even have real windows. No housing unit does. During the Great Famine, windows were considered security risks and they were eliminated from construction designs. Besides, we can't afford the luxury of using land for private gardens." He gave her a wry smile. "My picture window actually conceals a set of storage units."

"I'm sure it's a very practical approach," Ariel said politely, trying to sound enthusiastic. "The whole room is beautiful, and the view of the garden sets it off to perfection."

"But you wouldn't trade that perfect garden scene for a single window box of real petunias, would you?" Mac said.

"I guess not." She smiled apologetically. "After a while, I'd get so frustrated at not being able to reach out and touch all that beauty."

"I believe I understand what you mean," Mac said huskily. "When I am with you, Ariel, I find that I want very much to reach out and touch . . . all that beauty."

The tiny space between the two of them was suddenly charged with a tension so thick, she had trouble breathing. Or perhaps the tension had been there from the beginning, and had only now broken out of the secret places where they'd been keeping it hidden, even from themselves.

The cool, flower-scented air swirled around her, and the silence in the room grew oppressive, pulsing with each heavy beat of her heart. A whippoorwill called out from the make-believe garden, his cry astonishingly loud in the breathless quiet of their room, but neither of them stirred. Ariel knew that if she made even the smallest move toward Mac, he would take her into his arms and they would make love.

Or at least they would have sex. She could pretend they were making love, but of course there would be no real emotions flowing between them, however spectacular the sexual fireworks. And Ariel didn't doubt for a moment that there would be fireworks. Mac had a body that would provoke lustful fantasies in any woman whose blood pumped still through her veins. More important, he had an intelligence and sensitivity that had prompted her to see herself and her world in a whole new light. For the past few hours, he'd made her feel more fully alive, more aware of herself as a woman, than any man she'd ever known. But time was their enemy. They shared no past and they could look forward to no future. Despite the fact that she wanted to have sex with Mac more than she had ever wanted anything before, common sense demanded that she walk away from temptation before she got badly hurt. This was not the moment to indulge her deepest and most secret fantasy.

Mac spoke in the split second before she did the sensible thing and got up from the bed. "You are right in what you are thinking," he said, his voice taut. "There is no future for us to share, no friendship to build that will last us a lifetime. Does that mean we have nothing to give each other, no joyful memories we can create together here and now?"

"Memories are capricious creatures," Ariel said. "What if the memories we make turn out to be painful ones?"

"We won't let them be anything but happy. If you choose to join your body with mine, Ariel, I will see that you feel only pleasure. You have my promise."

"You're very sure of yourself, Mac." She smiled wistfully. "Has your world forgotten that sometimes the body can feel pleasure when the soul is feeling nothing but pain?"

"Have you forgotten that sorrow for chances lost makes the most painful memory of all?"

Ariel tore her gaze away from his. She looked down at his outstretched hands and knew that she would regret it for the rest of her life if she refused, just this once, to follow her instincts rather than the dictates of reason and common sense. When Mac returned to his own distant century, to his world of luxury illusion and overcrowded reality, she would have a lifetime ahead of her to be reasonable. For this one brief moment, she wanted to surrender to everything within herself that was wild and passionate and free. She wanted to find out what it was like to have torrid sex with the most fascinating man she'd ever met. She wanted, more than anything in the world, to have Mac make love to her.

She had no way to justify her decision, but right now, she didn't care about justification and logic. She lifted her head with a touch of defiance, meeting his gaze and putting her hands into his waiting clasp. "You're right, Mac," she said softly. "We should seize the moment while we can. Let's make sure we have lots of happy memories to take with us when we say goodbye."

For a moment, he didn't move. Then he slowly drew her toward him, carrying her hands to his lips and kissing the tip of each finger, one by one. It was a gesture of such profound respect, and such unexpected tenderness, she felt tears clog the back of her throat, as if the goodbyes she dreaded were already happening.

"No frowns, and no tears, is that agreed?" Mac brushed his thumbs across her eyelids. "For the next several minutes, melancholy thoughts are strictly forbidden."

She tried to smile. "All sexual partners will be cheerful. Is that another one of your tiresome government rules?"

"No, that one was strictly mine, but let's see what I can do to enforce regulations." He put his hands on her shoulders and pressed her down against the pillows, settling her against his hips so that she could feel the protective curve of his arm around her shoulders as well as the hard, urgent thrust of his arousal against her pelvis.

His heart thudded in a strong, slow beat as he slowly explored the curves and hollows of her body. She surrendered willingly to the powerful currents flowing between them, feeling none of the restraint and self-consciousness that, in the past, had always made her such an awkward and inhibited lover. He pushed her hair away from her face, tracing the outline of her eyes and cheeks with a wonder that suggested he found her exquisitely beautiful. Then he stripped off his shirt before stroking his hands over her breasts and reaching under her T-shirt to remove her bra.

His expert, skillful seduction stumbled to an abrupt halt as he wrestled with the recalcitrant clip. His face assumed an expression of almost comical dismay as his fingers fumbled with the unfamiliar hook and eye. Finally, he gazed down at her with a rueful smile.

"Okay, I admit defeat. Permapel is a lot easier to deal with than this. Could you please show a rank amateur how the fastening on this piece of clothing works? It's not the same as the one you were wearing in the shower."

She took his hands and guided him through the simple movements that released the front hook of her bra. "Now you're an expert," she said.

"Hmm, I think you are too optimistic. The closure on the garment covering your lower body—"

"The zipper on my shorts."

"Yes, the zipper. I regret to say that it looks as if it may present a high-level challenge to a man of my limited experience."

She unsnapped the fastener at her waist, and unzipped the shorts. "Cooperation is permitted," she said. "Even encouraged."

He slipped the shorts over her hips and down her legs. "This," he said huskily, "is much more fun than permapel." Then he pulled off her shirt and thrust the bra aside, bending down in a single swift movement to take one of her nipples into his mouth.

Ariel's smile vanished in that instant. The feel of his beard stubble on her skin was electric, the caress of his mouth and tongue a balm that soothed, and simultaneously jolted her nerve endings into a state of tantalizing arousal.

As Mac suckled, a yearning warmth started deep in the pit of her stomach, spiraling outward, turning to fire in her blood and a deep ache at the juncture of her thighs. She tried to tell him how good she felt, how much she liked what he was doing to her, but her words faded into a groan of garbled pleasure.

She waited with mounting impatience for him to kiss her on the mouth, but although he trailed kisses over every inch of her body, he scrupulously avoided touching his lips to any part of her face. In the end, desperate for his kiss, she put her hands on either side of his head and pulled him upward. She finally understood how kissing a lover on the mouth could seem the most intimate and emotional act of sexual foreplay, and she longed to share that intimacy with Mac.

He looked down at her, his eyes dilated and dark as night. "What do you want from me, Ariel?"

"Kiss me," she whispered.

He framed her face with hands that shook. "Are you sure?"

"Very sure."

"I want to kiss you," he said hoarsely, as if admitting to a dark sexual fantasy. "I want to feel your tongue touch mine at the same moment as my hand touches you here." His fingers moved between her legs, caressing her with a feather-lightness that sent sparks of fire blazing through her veins.

Her hips arched upward against his hand as Mac slowly bent his head to take possession of her mouth. She'd expected hot, fierce passion—she'd wanted hot, fierce passion—but his kiss was tender, achingly gentle, and stiff with restraint. Ariel flicked her tongue against his lips, teasing them apart, tempting and provoking, until Mac's hard-won control broke, and he slanted his mouth across hers, his tongue seeking her out with urgent passion.

The taste of him sizzled through Ariel's veins like brandy bursting into hungry blue flame. He deepened the kiss until she was dizzy with the slow advance and retreat of his tongue. The touch of his fingers became more sensual, more probing, feeding the heat that was building deep inside her. She stirred restlessly, trembling on the formless, shivery edge of release.

"Mac," she whispered, her breath coming in soft, heaving bursts. "Now. Please."

"Not yet, caressa."

Caressa. She registered the unfamiliar word, but she was too caught up in the demands of her body to stop and ask him what it meant. Blindly, she sought the waistband of his sweatpants, all hesitation and modesty long since burned away in the fire of her own longing. Her hand slid down the pulsing, throbbing length of his erection, and his groan of pleasure stirred a response deep inside her. Never in her life had she felt so sexy and so desirable. Never had she felt so uninhibited, so open and so free.

He spoke hoarsely, against her lips. "Ariel, you have to stop. You're taking me to the edge."

"I hope so," she murmured. "Because I'm already there."

Mac captured her hand and held it over her head, looking at her intently. "Yes, caressa, I believe you are." He shifted on the bed, pulling her under him and thrusting into her. Ariel closed her eyes, accepting the heavy fullness of him, welcoming him in. She could feel herself shimmering around him, trembling on the verge of a fulfillment so intense she could barely imagine its dimensions.

Mac touched her lightly on the cheek, and she opened her eyes. "Now," he whispered, his eyes glittering, his mouth taut. "Now we are both ready, I think."

For answer, she wrapped her legs around his hips, opening her body to him, offering him all the passion and fire she normally struggled so hard to repress.

He muttered something low and liquid-sounding that she couldn't understand. Then he put his mouth against hers, hot and wet and open. His arms tucked beneath her hips, holding her so tight against him that she could no longer tell where her body ended and his began. He thrust into her again, deep and hard, absorbing the hoarse pants of her breath and the scattered sighs of her delight.

She felt herself begin to unravel. One last kiss and she shattered around him, shaking and gasping, poised on the very edge of the precipice. But it seemed that Mac knew just how to prolong her climax, for he held her there, suspended in ecstasy, the world swirling around her in a blinding, shimmering haze.

And then, when the tremors of her release had almost stopped, he drove into her one final time. His body went rigid, his head went back, and as he climaxed, she peaked again, tumbling off the precipice in endless, exhilarating freefall.

Spent, exhausted, disoriented, Ariel clung to Mac for a long, silent moment. When he finally spoke, his voice was quiet, but with an edge of harshness. "It has never been like that for me before, Ariel."

The truth came with surprising ease. "Nor for me. It was wonderful, Mac. You were wonderful."

He put his hand on the flatness of her stomach, his fingers thrumming in a restless caress. "I wish that you could be my Silver Partner, Ariel." He looked out into the illusory garden, his expression bleak. "I wish that we could live together and that you could become the mother of my child."

There was absolutely no point in dwelling on the impossible, nothing to be gained from wishing for what could never be. Much better if she didn't answer, but the words came out of nowhere, or perhaps from the deepest and most honest corner of her soul. "I wish that, too," she said huskily. "I wish we could be together, Mac."

He rolled onto his side, taking her with him, holding her very close. "There is no way for me to take you back with me to my world," he said. "The time-travel chamber that sent Consuela and me here is able to receive back only those people it has already sent out."

Ariel avoided his gaze. "You could stay here," she said.

Mac put his hand under her chin and gently pulled her head around until she was forced to look at him. "No, caressa, I cannot stay here, much as I wish that I could. It is my duty to take Consuela back to my own time. She must face the bitter consequences of the murder she committed, and the havoc she wrought. The people of my country need to see that the death of their president has been avenged, that the killer has been brought to trial. My own wishes have no importance relative to what is at stake for my country."

Everything that he said was true, and Ariel would have admired him less if he'd felt any differently. She cleared her throat. "Yes, of course, I knew that, Mac." She tried to sound bright and cheerful. "I guess that means we need to get dressed and start thinking about how we're going to transport ourselves to Edwards, Colorado, without having the police and half the federal agents in the country hot on our tails."

Very gently, Mac pushed her back against the pillows. "That is indeed a major problem to be solved."

"Yes, and we should—"

"I think much more creatively when I'm lying down, don't you?" He slid his hand down her body, the movement casual, seemingly random, and entirely erotic.

Ariel wouldn't have believed there was an ounce of sexual energy left in her aching, replete body. Astonishingly, it seemed that she was wrong. Her thoughts scattered as Mac leaned over her, his head slowly descending for a kiss. "Mac, we can't . . . we don't have time—"

He pressed his finger to her mouth, silencing her. "This is the only time we will ever have that is just for us. Let's make every second count, Ariel. I'm going to need the memories."

9

MAC WAS PACING restlessly and Pip was projecting a list of names and dates onto the TV when Ariel came out of the shower. He gestured to the screen, freezing it on a picture of an attractive young woman in a neon-bright ski outfit.

"Who's she?" Ariel asked.

"Erika Johansen."

"She's pretty."

"She is much more than pretty," Mac said grimly. "She is of seminal importance in the twenty-first century. I was checking to see if Pip had any records of important people who lived in Edwards, Colorado, and her name came up immediately."

"What did she do?" Ariel asked.

"She was born in Edwards in 1965," Mac said. "She won a bronze medal for cross-country skiing in the 1988 winter Olympics, and she was elected to Congress for the first time in November, 1996."

Ariel shook her head, trying to orient herself to knowing the outcome of a congressional election that hadn't yet been held. Knowledge of an event in the very near future felt even more strange than hearing about events two centuries later. She glanced back at the television just as the image on the screen changed to a formal portrait of the same woman, taken at least two decades after the ski shot.

"She has an interesting face," Ariel said. "Obviously, you believe she's got something to do with Consuela's interest in Edwards?"

"I'm sure she has," Mac said, his voice bleak. "Erika Johansen is a very famous woman. Following her election in 1996, she had a brilliant career in government. After two terms in the House of Representatives, she was elected to the Senate, and then to the vice presidency. Eventually, she went on to become the first female president of the United States."

"Good heavens!" Fascinated, Ariel stared at the TV screen. "Was she a ..." She shook her head, getting her tenses straight. "Will she be a good president?"

"One of the best. She had outstanding leadership ability, and historians credit her with persuading American citizens to take the difficult steps that kept this continent relatively free of starvation during the years of the Great Famine."

If Consuela had decided to meddle in the events of the past, interfering in the life of the first female president of the United States certainly seemed like a good place to start. "Did Pip find any record of someone called Frances Foster?" Ariel asked.

He shook his head. "But I wouldn't expect to find her mentioned. After all, it's just an alias Consuela is using. Pip's data banks only contain the names of historical figures of great importance."

Ariel shivered, suddenly overwhelmed by the enormous responsibility she and Mac were carrying. "Do you think Consuela plans to harm Erika Johansen in some way?"

"It seems a distinct possibility," he said. "In view of her recent activities, I wonder if she is plotting another murder."

"But she couldn't succeed, could she?" Ariel asked. "I mean, history is history, right? You know that Erika Johansen became president, and Consuela must know the same thing. Doesn't that mean Consuela also knows that any attempt to murder Erika is doomed to failure?"

"I don't know," Mac said. "Consuela is the expert on time travel, not me. Perhaps she believes that the past can be altered in ways that have predictable effects on the future. Perhaps she has no plans to kill Erika, only to subvert her policies, or change them in some way to Consuela's advantage. I only know that you and I had better get ourselves to Colorado with all possible speed if we want to keep history chugging along the old fashioned way."

"We have more than nine hundred dollars," Ariel said. "That should be enough money for two plane tickets. And if it isn't, Pip can always get more."

Mac shook his head. "It's too risky for us to take a commercial flight. Pip scanned the news broadcasts while you were in the shower and showed me the relevant excerpts. You and I seem to have become overnight criminal sensations. I would say that, thanks to Consuela, we are by now the two most actively hunted people in the state."

Ariel paled. "How has she managed to achieve that?"

"By accusing us not only of conspiring to murder her, but also of cherishing the absurd belief that we are aliens from another planet with a mission to save America. In other words, the police think we're crazy enough to be dangerous."

Ariel wasn't impressed. "I can't think why they would. On days when the breeze is blowing in the right direction, half the citizens of Los Angeles think they're aliens from another planet."

"That may be. But according to the latest news reports, Consuela has convinced the authorities that we're plotting to capture the mayor of Los Angeles and hold him to ransom. The mayor has received threats, and there was an incident—the police aren't saying what—that caused a two-hour evacuation of city hall."

"A bomb threat?"

"Given that the authorities are keeping so quiet, I would guess Consuela cooked up something fancier than that. The police can't ignore us if we seem to be a major threat to public safety, particularly since they already have warrants out for our arrest on the charge of attempting to murder Consuela."

"She's been very clever," Ariel conceded. "A plan to capture the mayor of L.A. in order to save America sounds just kooky enough to be credible. Damn! She always seems to be two steps ahead of us."

Mac nodded. "And the police consider her a credible witness since several people think they saw me trying to kill her."

Ariel tossed the damp towel onto the bed. "Still, nobody who knows me could possibly believe that I'm involved in all that nonsense about space aliens, and plots to kidnap the mayor. I'm the biggest stick-in-the-mud this side of crocodile city."

"Are you sure?" Mac's voice was dry. "Your charming neighbor Brenda Lewinski announced to an assembly of breathless reporters that you have informed her many times that you have a secret lover who comes from a distant, mysterious location, and who is going to unite with you to change the course of world history."

"What? What did that idiot say?"

"That you have a secret lover who comes from a distant—"

Ariel slammed her fist on the rickety table hard enough to bounce Mac's can of soda onto the floor. She was so furious that she didn't even bother to pick it up. "Brenda's talking about that ridiculous seance she dragged me to, when some weirdo with bad breath put his hands on my head, went off into a fake trance and spouted all that garbage! I've never mentioned a lover to Brenda Lewinski, much less a mysterious one. I don't have a lover—"

"I am desolate to be forgotten so soon," Mac said, taking her hand and rubbing her bruised knuckles. "I had allowed myself to hope that you might remember me for at least the next week or two."

Her cheeks blazed. "I didn't mean you, Mac. I'll always remember... How could I forget what happened between us?"

"I'm glad, because I, too, will always remember our time together." He carried her hand to his lips, kissing it tenderly. "Does it not occur to you, caressa, that perhaps your weirdo with bad breath is not such a fake, after all? You do have a lover who comes from a faraway place, and I believe that finding Consuela Timmons and taking her back to my world will have a definite impact on our history. Do you not find it intriguing that your 'fake' clairvoyant should have seen so clearly into the future?"

Ariel drew in a sharp breath. "It's coincidence, Mac, nothing more. The guy was a total flake." She turned away, refusing to let words like *fate* and *destiny* pervert her last traces of common sense. She deliberately changed the focus of their discussion. "Well, the damage Brenda can do is limited, however much she runs off at the mouth. Thank heavens for permapel, that's all I can say. At least the police don't know what you look like—"

Mac picked up the empty soda can and tossed it with perfect aim into the trash basket on the far side of the room. "Unfortunately, they know exactly what I look like. They have an excellent photograph of me."

"How? Where from?" Ariel thought quickly. "Did someone snap you at the hospital? A security camera, maybe?"

He shrugged. "More likely the picture was provided courtesy of Consuela's Pip. She's given the police my name, a phony birth date and even a last-known address. She's obviously determined to have the authorities find us."

"How can you have a last-known address when you only arrived here yesterday?" Ariel asked.

"According to the records, I have been living on Orange Street, in Anaheim, for almost three years."

She gulped. "The hospital where Consuela was taken after the accident is right next door to Anaheim."

"Why do you sound surprised?" he asked. "Naturally, Consuela wants the police to concentrate their search in the area where she suspects us to be. You must remember, caressa, that whatever plans she has, we are the only people in my century or yours who offer any real threat to her success. Of course she wants to point the authorities in our direction."

"But the police will soon discover that you never lived on Orange Street, and then they're going to start doubting Consuela's story. In the long run, she's just throwing suspicion on herself—"

"No, she's not," Mac said, his expression savage. "You can be sure that, according to the records, everything Consuela reports about me is true."

Ariel ran her fingers through her hair, wishing she had a comb. Then she wondered why in the world she was bothering about snarls in her hair when there were about ten thousand more important things for her to worry about right now. "If Consuela can falsify the records, can't you correct them?"

"Not with this Pip," Mac said, tugging at the silver tube hanging around his neck in a rare show of frustration. "I'm guessing that Consuela must have an extremely powerful Pip implanted subdermally."

"Which means she has the power to do all sorts of things you can't do?" Ariel asked.

"Unfortunately, yes. I'm guessing that she's in possession of a Pip with a vast data base, carefully tailored to meet her specific needs in this time and place. I'm willing to bet that if we turn up at any public airport and try to board a plane, the police will be waiting for us, alerted by my so helpful former Silver Partner."

"My brother-in-law has a private jet, and a pilot's license," Ariel said. "He could fly us to Colorado and we wouldn't have to go anywhere near a commercial airline. That way, Consuela and the police might both lose track of us, don't you think?"

"Possibly, at least until we get within a certain range of her Pip. I will have to think of some way to block her capacity to pick up my retinal scan before we get too close to her." Mac began to look happier. "That's wonderful news about your brother-in-law, Ariel. I couldn't think of a way to get from here to Colorado without being caught."

"Except that we're stranded here in a crummy motel, and Ralph and his plane are miles away in San Clemente."

Mac conferred with Pip. "To be precise, your brother-in-law lives 36.27 kilometers from here, and we would have to drive along several highways that are significantly monitored by police persons in order to get to his housing unit. We need to devise some method of getting there without the police recognizing us. What a pity that people in your time wear masks only on Halloween."

"I absolutely, positively, refuse to steal any more cars," Ariel said. Much as she wanted to see Miranda again, and help find Consuela, she felt obligated to draw the moral line somewhere. "And besides, it's not just a question of getting to San Clemente and then everything will be easy. Ralph has his house wired like a fortress, with every electronic safety device you can ever imagine. We'd never be able to get to see him or my sister without triggering an alarm that would warn the entire town we were coming."

"Not true," Mac said, wiggling his neck chain. "This Pip is only a toy, but even a toy from my century is sufficiently powerful to disarm any electronic security system your century has devised. Trust me, Ariel, we can walk right into the heart of your brother-in-law's home without tripping a single alarm."

The possibility of actually seeing Miranda and getting help from Ralph was inducement enough to powerfully concentrate Ariel's mind. "Give me a few minutes to think about how we're going to get there, will you?" she said to Mac. "Maybe we could rent a car."

"Certainly," he said. "I take it that such a rental transaction can occur without your having to show any documentation?"

"No, of course you have to show a driver's license, but we have Consuela's fake one—" She subsided into silence as she realized the absurdity of her suggestion. She looked nothing like the picture on Consuela's fake license. Besides, the police would have given her description, and Mac's, to every rental-car agency in the state. If she tried to rent a car, the clerk would be alerting the police before the ink was dry on the paperwork.

"I guess we can't rent a car," she acknowledged, "but I'll think of something."

Mac got to his feet. "I'm sure you will," he said courteously. "And in the meantime, I believe that I will go for a short walk. My muscles are feeling cramped from lack of exercise."

"You can't go outside, someone will see you."

"I shall endeavor not to be recognized."

"Right. Good plan. There must be at least twenty-three people in Greater L.A. who haven't seen your picture. Feel free to stretch your muscles, secure in the knowledge that it may be five whole minutes before a squad car is sent after you."

Mac opened the door. "We must have transportation, Ariel," he said quietly. "I will be back soon."

"Mac, don't be an idiot. You can't go out!"

She spoke to the closed door, and when she wrenched it open and hobbled out into the parking lot, she couldn't see any trace of him. In the minute it had taken her to cross the room and open the door, Mac had vanished.

She wondered if the next time she saw him, he would be wearing handcuffs, in a TV news report.

She'd been pacing the room for fifteen minutes, her mood getting progressively blacker, when she heard the roar of an engine rounding the corner of the motel and zooming into the parking lot. With a reckless disregard for the laws of logic and probability, she decided Mac was returning, and flung open the door just in time to see a man wearing a leather jacket and a crash helmet with a black visor screech to a halt outside her door.

The biker put one sneakered foot to the ground and steadied the bike. He held out a second helmet and leather jacket. "Want a ride to San Clemente?" he asked.

"Mac? Oh my God, Mac!"

"It might be a good idea if we left quite quickly," he said, pressing the helmet and jacket into her hands. "Before this vehicle is reported stolen."

"I can't believe you did this! I specifically asked you not to steal any more cars!" He was still holding out the clothes, so she shoved her arms into the jacket and buckled the helmet strap around her chin.

"But this isn't a car," he protested. "Pip assured me that the engine technology of the motorcycle is significantly different from that of the previous vehicles we have—um—borrowed. Besides, the headpieces with the black visors provide most excellent disguises. I couldn't resist."

"Unfortunately, they only provide so-so protection against getting your skull cracked open in an accident."

"Pip has already warned me of that. However, we shall not have an accident."

"Hah! Is that based on your years of driving experience?" She adjusted the mouthpiece built into the crash helmet, swung her leg over the bike and sat down behind Mac, refusing to admit to herself that she'd always wanted to roar down the highway on a giant Harley. "What happened to the owners of this bike?" she demanded.

"They are sleeping peacefully on the steps of a restaurant. They will certainly be discovered soon, which is yet another reason for us to hurry."

"How in the world did you even manage to drive the bike this far?"

He kicked the starter. "Pip has written a most helpful guidance program, based on observations of your own driving techniques. Pip instructs me as we go. Now that I realize vehicles in your century have no self-guidance mechanism, we should have no problems."

"Pip is giving you directions as we go? Oh, boy! Now I'm feeling real confident."

Mac opened the throttle and the engine revved up. "I am so glad your worries have been alleviated, caressa."

She put her arms around his waist. "Do you, by any chance, know what's meant by heavy irony, Mac?"

"Certainly." She heard the laughter in his voice. "Do you?"

Ariel realized that the strange fizzing sensation in her veins wasn't fear. It was happiness. Her breath caught for a moment in her throat. Then she laughed, just as if she wasn't about to tool down twenty miles or so of freeway, behind a man who'd probably never even seen a motorbike until half an hour ago, with the entire California Highway Patrol ready to jump on their tail.

"I'm ready," she said. "Let's get out of here."

As Mac spun the bike around, she got a glimpse of herself reflected in the window of their abandoned motel room. The black helmet made her look mysterious, alien. But her body language spoke of a woman who was bold, reckless and one hundred percent alive. She visualized herself two days earlier, worrying about what she was going to wear to Miranda's Halloween party and damn near smothering in her own inhibitions. It was hard to believe the two women were one and the same person.

As they roared out of the motel parking lot, Ariel decided she liked this new woman a whole lot better than the old one.

10

THEY DITCHED the Harley a couple of hundred yards from the main entrance to Miranda and Ralph's house, and went on foot to within twenty feet of the heavy, wrought-iron gates. They were closed, chained and padlocked, with signs warning in both English and Spanish that the gates and surrounding fence were weight-and-pressure sensitive. Ariel knew that the signs didn't lie. Rattle the gates too hard, and an alarm would sound. Climb the fence, ditto.

"At least the reporters seem to have packed up and gone home," she said, huddling in the shadows of a piñon pine, where they had taken cover. "I guess the police can't afford the manpower to stake out the place twenty-four hours a day just on the off chance that we'll turn up here."

Mac held Pip close to his ear. "Pip doesn't detect any human presence within a fifty-meter radius of where we're standing," he reported.

"The road doesn't go anywhere except to Miranda and Ralph's house," she said. "At this time of night, there shouldn't be any traffic."

"Then Pip and I will start work on the deactivation of the alarm system."

Mac and Pip engaged in an exchange of low-voiced Spanglish dialogue. Heavy clouds scudded across the moon, and Ariel shivered, shoving her hands deep into the pockets of her stolen leather jacket. One day, when this was all over, she was going to have to do some detective work of her own and find out how she could compensate all the people who'd made unwitting donations to the cause of saving the world from Consuela Timmons. Somewhere in Anaheim, there was probably a cold—and very angry—biker.

"The system is deactivated," Mac announced.

As far as Ariel was concerned, the whole process seemed much too easy, even for a micro-minicomputer from the twenty-second century. She'd been there when Ralph had demonstrated just a few of his whiz-bang security gadgets, and it didn't seem likely that a couple of minutes of burping and humming from Pip would have taken care of everything.

"Are you sure there aren't a few secret trip wires Pip didn't notice?" she asked. "Remember, the system's tied into the local police station, so it's all over for us if we set off an alarm."

"I am sure. And we don't have to worry about the police noticing the system is cut off. Pip is sending out a false monitoring signal so that they will have no idea the system is deactivated."

She hadn't even thought of that wrinkle, which wasn't surprising given that her experiences in criminal activity were limited to bailing her parents out of jail after one of their numerous save-the-earth protests, and producing a public-service documentary on women in prison. Information she sincerely hoped she would never have to utilize personally.

"How many people are inside the house?" she asked. "Do we know?"

"Pip indicates that there are two humans sleeping in a room on the second floor, southwest corner of the house," Mac said. "There are also two people sleeping on the opposite side of the house, same floor."

"That'll be the housekeeper and handyman. They live in a two-bedroom apartment over the garage. If we're reasonably quiet, they'll never hear us."

"We can't go in through the gate," Mac said. "It's floodlit and in direct line of sight from both bedrooms. Pip could destroy the lights, but he can't open the padlocks. Unfortunately, they're manually controlled, not electronic. To open them, we'd need a tool that can saw through steel."

"Then how are we going to get in?" Ariel asked.

Mac's expression became suspiciously cheerful. "Over the fence."

"Over the fence?" Ariel eyed the twelve-foot stucco wall, which barely had footholds for a centipede, let alone a human. "Sure, Mac, why not? But if you're planning to take a running leap and fling yourself over the top, I guess I should point out that the wall is about seven feet too high for me to do the same."

"I will lift you up," Mac said. "You must grab on to the top of the wall, pull yourself up and then sit and wait for me to help you down on the other side."

Good grief, the crazy man really was planning to take a running leap over the wall! He picked her up before she had time to point out all the potential problems with that lunatic scenario. He carried her over to the wall and swung her into a sitting position on his shoulders. It was immediately apparent that however high she stretched, if she stayed sitting on Mac's shoulders, she was never going to reach the top of the wall.

"Can you stand?" he asked. "I will have to hold on to your ankles to support you as you reach for the top of the wall. Can you tolerate the pain to your ankle?"

Of course she couldn't. She was the world's biggest coward. The dentist wasn't allowed to even look at her, much less touch her, without giving her an injection first.

"Yes." She swallowed a giant gulp of air. "Let's do it now, Mac. Quickly."

Without comment, Mac helped her clamber into a standing position on his shoulders. She bit down on her knuckles and waited for the shooting pain in her ankle to subside enough for her to talk. "What next?"

"Just like I explained. Reach out and you will be able to grab the top of the wall. Swing yourself up. Then wait until I've made it to the other side, and I will help you to jump down."

Mac was planning to make a twelve-foot leap over the damn wall, and she wasn't sure she could pull herself eighteen inches or so onto the top of it. Ariel gritted her teeth, ignoring the excruciating pain in her ankle. No way was she going to admit that she didn't have the strength to heave herself onto the top of the damn wall. With grim determination, she hauled herself up, and straddled the wall, panting triumphantly.

"Great going," Mac said softly. "Now it's my turn."

He jogged back to the far side of the road, before turning and confronting the twelve-foot stucco barrier. Since he appeared unperturbed, Ariel's stomach decided to feel sick for him. A flying leap that missed would be a real easy way for Mac to get himself killed.

He stretched his hands over his head, flexed his muscles, drew in a couple of deep breaths, then bent into a semi-crouching position, before running full tilt at the wall, his body uncoiling as he gathered speed. With a leap of such sheer animal grace that it stopped Ariel's breath, he hurled his body up and over the wall, clearing the top by a fraction of an inch, and landing on the other side with his head tucked into his hands, and his knees balled against his chest.

Her heart only started beating again when he uncurled himself and slowly stood up. "The landings are a hell of a lot easier when you're wearing permapel," he said, plucking blades of grass from his sweatpants and giving her a reassuring grin.

It was an odd moment to realize that she'd fallen in love. Ariel stared down at him, and felt her eyes burn with hot tears. She scrubbed them away with the heel of her hand, mumbling something about pollen and hay fever. "I hope you didn't split those sweatpants," she grumbled. "They're my dad's favorites."

"The pants are fine," he said. "How about you?"

"Peachy keen." *Sure I'm fine. If you don't count the fact that you're going to break my heart when you leave me.*

Mac took a couple of paces back. "Are you ready to jump off that wall?"

She managed a carefree smile. "Sure. Are you ready to catch me?"

His answering smile gleamed in the moonlight. "You are brave tonight, caressa."

She gave an airy wave of her hand. "Compared to the roof of my town house, this fence is a piece of cake, right?"

"Right," he said, looking amused. "A mere four-meter nothing." He held out his arms. "Ready when you are, caressa."

Ignoring the whirligig spinning in her stomach, she stood up on top of the wall and launched herself toward Mac. His arms felt strong and steady and achingly familiar when he caught her.

"Well done," he said softly. "A great jump. You are very courageous, Ariel."

Only when you're around. She turned away, afraid of what he might read in her face. "Thanks," she said quickly. "You can put me down now, Mac."

He set her carefully on her feet, but he didn't let her go. Instead, he cupped her face in his hands and stared into her betrayingly bright eyes. "Why are you crying?" he asked quietly. "And do not repeat your nonsense about allergies. What is wrong, caressa?"

"Nothing's wrong." She spoke with determined briskness. "We need to hurry, Mac. We've got to find Miranda and Ralph if we're going to save the world before morning."

Surprisingly, he didn't argue with her. He gave her one long, final look, then brushed his thumbs very lightly across her mouth. "How is your ankle? Can you walk, or shall I carry you?"

"I can walk. Pip's latest miracle cure seems to be holding up."

"Let us go, then."

Ariel knew that she ought to be grateful that he hadn't pushed for a more adequate explanation of her sudden tears. Instead, she couldn't resist asking him a question of her own. "You keep calling me caressa," she said as he strode across the lush, manicured lawn toward the house. "It sounds nice, but what does it mean?"

He didn't stop walking and he didn't look back. "I believe there is no accurate translation."

"An approximate one would do."

He covered several more yards of lawn before he swung around and answered her. "Caressa means beloved," he said. "It is a word I have never used before in any language."

He turned his back on her again without waiting to see her reaction, and carried on walking toward the house with swift silent steps.

Ariel felt the sudden painful constriction in her lungs and wondered if that might be the first sign of a heart that was slowly breaking.

The kitchen door was bolted on the inside with a simple old-fashioned metal bar that entirely defeated Pip's skills. "We'll have to break a window," Ariel said.

"That's easy enough." Mac took off his jacket, made a fist inside it and punched out a pane of glass. Despite her lingering fear that parts of the security system might still be operational, no alarms sounded, and it took only a matter of seconds for him to slide open the window and crawl inside. He lifted Ariel in after him.

"Give me directions," Mac said as they left the kitchen. "You know where your sister's bedroom is located."

"The stairs are through that door," she said, pointing him in the direction of the foyer. Built-in night-lights glowed in the baseboards, making their journey easier, and their route self-evident. Her sneakered feet making almost no sound, Ariel limped across the vast hallway toward the elegant central staircase.

Suddenly, Mac flung out his arm, shoving her behind him. "Don't move," he said. "Keep back."

"What is it?" Peering over his shoulder, she saw that Ralph was poised in the middle of the stairs, scraggy bare legs sticking out from beneath his bathrobe, his knobby ankles and big toes comically illuminated in the glow of the baseboard night-lights. There was, however, nothing comical about the large hunting rifle aimed squarely between Mac's eyes.

"Ralph!" she squeaked, and would have rushed forward if Mac hadn't held her with an iron grip. "Ralph, it's me, Ariel! For heaven's sake, put the gun away. Somebody could get hurt!"

Her brother-in-law gave not the slightest sign that he'd heard her. He kept his gaze fixed squarely on Mac. "Put your hands on your head and lie down on the floor," he said. "One wrong move and I'll shoot."

To the best of Ariel's knowledge, Ralph wouldn't be able to hit the side of a barn at twenty paces. But she didn't necessarily find that knowledge comforting since his trigger finger looked more than a touch shaky. Lord knew what he might hit if he got spooked.

Mac hesitated for a second, then obviously reached the same conclusion. Clearly deciding that this wasn't the moment for heroics, he linked his hands at the back of his head, and lay down on the marble floor.

Ariel took a couple of steps forward around his prone body. "Ralph, I'm sorry we couldn't call or any—"

"Get back," he ordered her, voice flat, the rifle jerking ominously. "Put your hands on your head and lie down next to your friend."

His voice dripped venom. Too astonished to obey, Ariel stared at him in shocked disbelief. "My God, Ralph, it's me. What's the matter with you? Put down that stupid gun before someone gets hurt."

"I know who you are," he said harshly. "It's what you are that I'm not sure about."

His words were like a blow to Ariel's gut. "I'm your friend, Ralph. I thought you were mine, too."

"If you weren't Miranda's sister, I'd shoot you and to hell with the consequences," Ralph said. "Now get down on the floor." His voice was so thick with bitterness that Ariel slid into a cross-legged sitting position next to Mac, not because she was obeying Ralph, but because her legs were threatening to give out on her. She saw that Mac was angling his Pip toward Ralph and bit her lip, forcing back her instinctive murmur of warning. She trusted Mac not to hurt her brother-in-law.

Mac gave a command to Pip and a wall of fire sprang up around Ralph, all the more terrifying in its total and complete unexpectedness. Ralph gave a hoarse shout, and Ariel instinctively recoiled, expecting to be singed by a blast of heat, but the temperature didn't change and she realized with a giant surge of relief that the fire was no more than one of Pip's illusions.

"Stay down!" Mac yelled and hurled himself forward. Through the haze and flicker of flames and smoke, she saw him bring Ralph down in a flying tackle. The rifle went off as Mac snatched it from Ralph's hands, shooting a bullet into the chandelier and sending shards of glass spattering over the hall.

The instant Mac had possession of the rifle, the fire vanished. Ralph made a rush at the gun, but Mac held him off with one hand, holding the rifle high over his head, out of Ralph's reach. Obviously realizing that he was hopelessly outmatched, Ralph sat on the bottom step, nursing his bruises and staring straight ahead, showing no more emotion than if fires routinely appeared and disappeared in his hallway, leaving behind no trace of their existence. No wonder he'd acquired such a reputation for success in the world of high-stakes, international finance, Ariel thought with wry admiration. It must take nerves of steel, and a certain type of courage, to reveal no shock, and no fear in this situation.

With surprising efficiency, Mac unloaded the rifle. "Where did you learn to do that?" Ariel asked, walking over to sit down on the step next to Ralph.

Mac dropped the bullets into the pocket of his leather jacket. "Graduate school. We had to take a couple of elective courses in the history of criminology, and I chose one on ancient weapons."

"Good choice. Bet you never thought it would come in so useful."

Mac propped the rifle against the wall. "I could wish that my skill had never been needed," he said. "Mr. Dunnett, I apologize for entering your home uninvited—"

"You are not an uninvited guest," Ralph said, tight-lipped. "You are a criminal trespasser."

"Ralph, let me explain." Ariel took hold of her brother-in-law's hand. With cool deliberation, he shook off her clasp.

She tried not to feel hurt. "Ralph, I don't know what you think is going on here, but Mac and I have done nothing wrong." She blushed as she remembered the stolen cars. "Well, almost nothing wrong. And we've been counting on you and Miranda to help us. Ralph, we need your assistance if we're going to prevent a terrible crime."

His stony expression gave way to a look of withering contempt. "I don't help terrorists."

Ariel blinked. "Terrorists?" she repeated stupidly. "What terrorists?"

"The FBI has spent the best part of the day here," Ralph said. "We are fully informed about your friend and his gang of thugs. We know what they're trying to do."

"Ralph, you've got this all wrong. Mac doesn't have anything to do with a gang of thugs. He doesn't know a soul in this world except me—"

"Is that what he told you?" Ralph's words dropped like shards of ice. "Ariel, I want to believe you're just a naive victim and not a fellow conspirator, but you've never struck me as a woman who'd be easy to deceive. Do you truly have no idea what this man is really planning to do? Don't you understand that he's threatened to poison the L.A. water supply and he has the technology to do it—"

"Oh my God!" Mac and Ariel exchanged horrified glances.

"Consuela," he said.

"Consuela," she agreed. "Damn!"

"She has been very busy, hasn't she?" Mac sighed. "Mr. Dunnett, we need to talk. Again, please accept our apologies for breaking into your home, but unfortunately we felt we had no other choice. I assure you, we have absolutely no criminal intentions of any sort, much less a plan to poison the citizens of this city. In fact, Ariel and I are in acute need of your assistance if we are to prevent a terrible tragedy that we believe is being plotted in Colorado."

Ralph's gaze flickered but he said nothing.

Ariel stood up, fists balling in frustration. "I don't know what's gotten into you, Ralph, but there sure doesn't seem to be much point in talking to you right at the moment. Frankly, I think it's pretty sad that you and I have been friends for three years, but an afternoon with the FBI is all it takes to convince you I'm some sort of political kook, with an agenda that involves threatening harm to millions of innocent people. Come on, Mac. We need to find Miranda. She'll be willing to help us, I know."

Ralph scrambled to his feet, his face whiter than before. "Stay away from Miranda, and I'll consider doing a deal with you. What do you want, Ariel? Money? I can get it for you. Transportation for you and your lover? Take whatever car you want—"

"Ralph, stop! This is horrible. I can't stand to hear you talk this way!" Ariel realized she was clutching her brother-in-law's robe, shaking him in sheer angry frustration. "How can you possibly believe that I'd ever hurt Miranda? She's my sister, and I love her! The way you're behaving is sick, Ralph, totally sick!"

"Don't, caressa. Don't allow yourself to be so upset." Mac put his arm around her. "You know the kind of lies Consuela tells and the proof she is capable of providing. You shouldn't blame your brother-in-law—"

"Yes, I should!" Ariel felt close to tears. "He ought to know that I would never in a million years do anything to harm Miranda." She shook off Mac's restraining arm. "This is ridiculous. I'm going to see my sister right now, and let her know that I'm alive. You two can do whatever you damn well please."

Ralph tried to stop her, but she astonished herself by pushing her elbow backward into his ribs so that he tripped and fell off the step. She stalked past him while he was still doubled up, clutching his gut and shaking his head.

Her ankle, thank heavens, didn't give out on her, and she ran up the stairs, hiccuping from the effort of not bursting into tears. She stormed into her sister's bedroom, and marched over to the king-size bed. She pulled out the earplugs her sister always wore when she was sleeping, and flipped up Miranda's trademark white velvet eye mask.

"Miranda, wake up! It's me, Ariel."

Miranda stirred groggily, then sat up, her gown of gossamer-fine lace and silk slipping from her shoulders. At the sight of her sister, her beautiful, sensuous mouth stretched into a wide, ecstatic smile.

"Ariel, sweetie! You're safe! I'm not dreaming, am I?" Miranda bounced off the bed and enfolded her sister in a bear hug. "God, I was so worried some fool of a cop would plug a bullet into you and stop to ask questions later. What in the world is going on with you, sweetie?"

"I'm saving the world, going crazy or plotting a terrorist attack. Pick one."

Miranda leaned back on her heels. "That's a no-brainer. Where my little sister's concerned, it has to be that you're saving the world. Of course, you do seem to be going about the task of salvation in a rather odd way."

Ariel's smile was shakier than she would have liked. "Where were you when the FBI was warning Ralph that I'm a terrorist out to end civilization as we know it?"

"Sweetie, that pompous little FBI squirt was talking such nonsense, it was all I could do not to laugh in his face. You surely didn't expect me to believe that you had become a political terrorist?"

"Ralph listened." Ariel couldn't quite filter the hurt from her voice. "He believed them."

Miranda squeezed her hand. "Well, honey, give the guy a break. He's only a man, after all."

Ariel heard something in her sister's voice that she'd never noticed before. "You love Ralph," she said. "You're really in love with him, aren't you?"

Miranda gave her a quizzical look. "Is that a major surprise? Why else did you think I married him?"

Ariel blushed. "Ah," Miranda said dryly. "His money. His millions and millions of dollars. I knew what everyone else thought, but I hoped you knew both of us better than that."

Ariel grimaced ruefully. "I seem to have made a lot of mistakes in judgment recently."

"Then you should understand why Ralph's being such an idiot," Miranda said. "I told him he was making a total horse's rear end out of himself, but he's basically had slightly less sense than a sand lizard ever since I told him I was pregnant."

"You're going to have a baby?" Ariel plunked down on the bed, staring at her sister in dazed delight. "Are you pleased?"

"Not a baby. Two babies. Twins, actually. And we're thrilled. I've been trying to get pregnant for two years. I was going to let you in on the secret the other night, but you sort of disappeared before I could."

"Oh, Lord, Miranda, twins! I can't believe it, this is such good news!" Misty-eyed, Ariel was just about to hug her sister, when Mac strode into the bedroom with Ralph slung over his shoulder. He dumped him on the bed without ceremony.

"God knows what your brother-in-law thought I planned to do, Ariel, but he insisted on fighting me when I tried to follow you upstairs. I tried not to hurt him, but it was impossible to avoid blacking his eye. Pip is working on it now, in an effort to reduce the swelling."

"I think he was trying to defend his wife," Ariel said. "He loves her a great deal, you know."

"Hah! Love. Your century uses that emotion as an excuse for everything." Mac scowled ferociously at Miranda. "You must be Ariel's sister, since you look so much like her. I cannot understand why you and your husband find it necessary to make her cry. It is clear to me that we have been mistaken in coming here to seek your assistance—"

Ariel hastily intervened. "Miranda didn't hurt my feelings, Mac. The opposite, in fact. She told me some great news. She's going to have twins, isn't that wonderful?"

Mac's scowl disappeared like magic. "Twin babies?" he said, smiling at her. "How wonderful for all of you! I met a set of identical twins once. It was a most extraordinary experience. As you can imagine, there are very few twin conceptions permitted in my world." He bowed politely. "I offer you my most sincere felicitations, Mrs. Dunnett."

"Thank you." Miranda's gaze was somewhere between amused and awed as she took in the muscular details of Mac's appearance. "Would you mind telling me what this is all about, Mr. . . . er . . . Are you really the Robert Macmillan the FBI has been warning us about for the past two days?"

"My name is Robert Macmillan, and I am sure the FBI has been warning you about me, although I doubt if I would recognize myself in the descriptions they have given you."

Ariel noticed that Ralph was edging toward the foot of the bed. It seemed that Mac noticed it, too. "The panic alarm button that you are seeking, Mr. Dunnett, has been deactivated. As have all the phones and telecommunications equipment in the house. There is absolutely no way for you to make contact with anyone outside this room."

Ralph's gaze slid for a betraying moment to the TV monitor in the corner of the room, which displayed nothing but a dead, blank screen.

"Don't be deceived by that monitor, Mr. Dunnett. Neither the police nor your security service have any idea your alarm system has been turned off." Mac's voice was coolly informative. "Would you like me to show you the pictures your security firm believes it is receiving of the exterior of your house?"

Without waiting for Ralph's answer, he spoke briefly to Pip. The TV monitor flickered to life with a view of the front door, followed by shots of various sections of the house, including a clear picture of a field mouse, apparently running across the sill of an unbroken kitchen window.

Ralph finally showed some emotion. He reached into the pocket of his robe and pulled out a handkerchief, which he used to dab at the sweat breaking out on his upper lip. Even Miranda looked shaken, and her hand crept out to find her husband's. "How did you do that?" she asked Mac.

"Manipulation of electronic data," he said. "The technology is merely an extension of systems you already use every day in your society."

"What do you want from us?" Ralph asked Mac. "Why do you need to subject my wife to this sort of stress? If you're going to kill us, just go ahead and do it."

"For goodness' sake, Ralph, stop being such a total jerk," Ariel said. "Of course we're not planning to kill you! In fact, we wouldn't have involved you if we'd been able to think of any other way to get where we have to go."

"Where's that?" Miranda asked.

"Colorado," Ariel said.

"What for?" Ralph persisted.

Mac broke in before Ariel could speak. "We'll tell you that when you've agreed to help us."

"I don't help people break the law." Ralph tightened the belt of his robe. "Ariel, listen to me. Turn yourself in to the authorities before it's too late. Do you have any idea what this man is really trying to do?"

"Yes," she said wryly. "I understand exactly what he's trying to do. He wants to stop Consuela Timmons from murdering the president."

"The president?" Miranda exclaimed. "Our president?"

Ralph shook his head. "This is pathetic, Ariel. Has this man really convinced you that Consuela Timmons wants to murder the president of the United States?"

"Sort of," she said. "Consuela doesn't want to murder *our* president. We believe she's planning to harm Erika Johansen, who hasn't been elected to Congress yet, but one day she's going to become the first female president of the United States—"

Miranda's smile faded. She reached out and took hold of her sister's hand. "Look, sweetie, I know these past few months have been tough and the last couple of days must have been real killers—"

"Not particularly," Ariel said tightly. "I'm not crazy, you know."

Miranda squeezed her sister's hand. "Then you must realize how irrational you sound when you talk like that, sweetie."

Of course she did, Ariel thought gloomily. The total impossibility of explaining to Ralph and her sister that Mac was a time traveler who considered the twenty-first century a part of history, suddenly dawned on her, full force. She turned to Mac. "Please, help me out here, could you?"

Mac smiled at her, his gaze oddly tender. "You know, caressa, I have discovered that when all else fails, it is sometimes a smart move to draw in a deep breath and tell the truth. So that is what I shall do. Here is the truth, Mr. Dunnett. Ariel and I need to get to Edwards, a small town in the mountains of Colorado, where the Johansen family lives. Erika

Johansen is currently running for election to the Congress of the United States and she will win the election. Furthermore, she will, in the year 2020, become president of this country. She will serve for two terms and be considered one of the greatest presidents since the days of Abraham Lincoln. I believe that Consuela Timmons intends to cause harm to Erika Johansen, most likely to murder her in an effort to change history. Ariel and I are trying to prevent that murder."

Miranda's mouth dropped open, and Ralph's expression changed from anger to impatient pity. "Mr. Macmillan, if you really fear there's a conspiracy to murder this Erika Johansen, I recommend that you leave the experts to take care of it. If Consuela Timmons is planning to murder a friend of yours, you should contact the FBI and tell them your story..."

"I am the FBI," Mac said curtly. "The head of it, in fact."

Miranda looked at her sister, her gaze sad. "Ariel," she murmured. "Help him. Tell him to turn himself in. We'll see that he gets good lawyers and the psychiatric help he needs..."

"Mac isn't crazy any more than I am," Ariel said, trying to sound her most composed and rational. "I'm absolutely sure he's the head of the United Bureau of Criminal Investigation for the United Republic of the Americas, just as he claims to be."

Ralph frowned. "You know perfectly well that there's no such organization. The man's playing you for a fool, Ariel, and you seem to be aiding and abetting his game."

She risked a glance at Mac and was only a little bit surprised to see that he was trying hard not to laugh. "If you think it's so damn funny, you explain." She spoke crossly, but in fact she was suddenly aware that the whole situation did have a faintly comical side to it.

Mac took her hand, and tucked it comfortably into his. "What Ariel is finding so difficult to tell you, Mr. Dunnett, is that I am a time traveler from the future, and that in the year 2196, which is where I have come from, the countries of North and South America have united to form a single republic, and I have the honor to be the head of that republic's Bureau of Criminal Investigation."

Miranda looked at Ariel and gave a small, uncertain laugh. "Okay, now I understand. This is a joke, right?"

"In very bad taste." Ralph failed to look even marginally amused. "This is a serious situation, Ariel, and bad jokes about time travel are way out of line."

She drew in a shaky breath. "Mac wasn't joking, Ralph. He's traveled back from the twenty-second century because he's chasing Consuela Timmons, who assassinated their president and then fled back in time to escape capture. And Mac needs to catch her soon, not only so that she can stand trial in her own century, but so that she can't start to plan any more mischief in ours."

"And this is the explanation that's supposed to persuade me to lend you my plane?" Ralph said with deadly quiet. "Good God almighty, Ariel, the FBI showed us film of your precious Mac meeting with Saddam Hussein! They've got wiretaps that link him to half a dozen terrorist groups operating in this country. And you're asking me to believe that he's a time-traveling cop come back to arrest a presidential assassin! Have you gone stark, staring mad?"

"The tapes you saw are nothing but clever fakes," Ariel said.

Ralph snorted. "Yeah, the FBI's framing innocent citizens, right? They do it all the time. Which paranoid group have you joined? The FBI are the good guys, Ariel."

"I don't think for a minute that the FBI frames innocent people," she said. "And I'm sure the police have excellent reason to think the tapes are genuine, but they're not." Ariel turned to Mac, her despair at the impossibility of convincing Ralph of the truth lifting as she wondered if this time, Consuela might have been just a bit too smart for her own good.

"Let's show them how easy it is to cook the evidence," she said. "Could Pip show us a tape of you and Ralph meeting with somebody who's already dead. How about President Nixon?"

Ralph looked irritated. "I never met President Nixon—"

"That's the whole point," Ariel said. "Mac?"

"Certainly Pip can do it." Mac gave Pip a set of instructions. For a full minute, nothing happened, then the TV hummed, and the Oval Office at the White House appeared on-screen. President Nixon, austere and dignified in a navy blue suit, worked at his desk. An aide knocked at the door and announced that Mr. Robert Macmillan and Mr. Ralph Dunnett were waiting to see him.

President Nixon rose to his feet, smiling courteously. Mac, wearing his sweatpants, and Ralph, barefoot and wearing his dressing gown, walked into the Oval Office and shook hands with the president. Everyone chatted agreeably about the weather, and the chances of the Washington Redskins winning the Superbowl. Neither the president nor any of his aides made any comment on the unsuitable clothes that Ralph and Mac were wearing.

"Have you seen enough?" Mac asked as the screen faded to black.

"It was interesting trick photography," Ralph said, his face a little pale. "I don't know how you did it, but the FBI would know at once it was faked."

"Of course," Mac agreed. "Because I deliberately set it up to appear ridiculous. I could just as easily have clothed the two of us in business suits and made it seem very real. Here, let me show you." He spoke to Pip again, and the identical scene was replayed, only this time both Mac and Ralph wore navy blue pinstripes, their hair was styled with 1970s side-burns and they both looked young enough to be college students.

"An interesting magic trick," Ralph said when the film clip ended.

"The same sort of magic trick Consuela Timmons performed for the FBI," Mac said quietly. "I hope you now understand how easy it is for people from my century to create visual lies. The fire I created downstairs was simply another example."

"What fire are you talking about?" Miranda asked.

"Not a real one," Mac said. "Don't be alarmed and I'll show you." He created a bonfire that surged sickeningly around Ariel, but doused the flames at Miranda's first horrified gasp.

"It's okay, I don't even feel warm, much less burned," Ariel said, moving to sit next to her sister on the king-size bed.

Ralph finally unbent sufficiently to ask a question. "What are you using to create these illusions?" he asked. "Show me the technology you're using."

Mac touched his Pip, which gave a dazzling little display of dancing laser lights. "This is what I used," he said. "We call it a Pip, which means Personal Information Provider. It's what you in your century might call a micro-minicomputer and it can be programmed to perform a range of different tasks. The Pip I have with me, unfortunately, is not provided with a very useful data base, since it was designed as an entertainment device. The one I suspect Consuela Timmons has implanted beneath her skin carries programs and information powerful enough to control and alter the electronic data banks of your entire government system."

Ralph put his arm around Miranda's shoulders and she leaned her head against him, clearly shaken. She drew in a long, taut breath. "Ralph, don't you think maybe we need to start this conversation over?"

"Yes, I think maybe we do." Ralph glowered at Mac. "Okay, tell me again exactly how you got here and what you claim is going on. From the beginning. Don't leave anything out."

"And then you'll consider letting us use your plane to fly to Colorado?" Ariel said.

"I'll give it serious consideration," Ralph said. "Now, Mr. Macmillan. Starting from the top."

11

RALPH NOT ONLY OWNED an eight-seater jet, but it turned out that he'd also recently bought a ski lodge on Beaver Creek Mountain where Mac and Ariel could stay while they searched for Consuela. Having finally been persuaded that Consuela Timmons was a twenty-second-century assassin, engaged in a nefarious plot to alter the progress of world history, Ralph was now determined to do his part in thwarting her plans. So great was his enthusiasm for hands-on involvement in bringing Consuela to justice, that Mac and Ariel were forced to spend most of the three-hour flight from San Clemente to Eagle-Vail airport convincing him that he wouldn't be helping if he set squadrons of private detectives to the task of searching for Consuela Timmons and the supposed Frances Foster.

At first, Miranda insisted on going with them, and had only been convinced to stay home when Mac pointed out that the high altitude and lack of oxygen would be detrimental to the twins at this stage of her pregnancy. Before he issued the warning, Mac had been smart enough to have Pip show her a color movie of her two unborn babies, nestled within her womb, one of them sucking his barely formed thumb, the other kicking his feet. When Pip also informed her that chromosomal analysis revealed the twins to be healthy, nonidentical boys, Miranda had become putty in Mac's hands. Ariel left her viewing the movie clip for the umpteenth time, and simultaneously checking the contents of her vast wardrobe, trying to decide which outfit to wear when she informed the FBI that her husband had left on an urgent business trip to Colorado, and no, the trip had absolutely nothing to do with the disappearance of her sister. In the face of such an unlikely story, her acting skills were clearly going to be tested to the limit.

Ralph had arranged for a chauffeur-driven limo to meet them at the Eagle-Vail airport in Colorado, which struck Ariel as a strangely luxurious form of transportation for two wanted fugitives. But Ralph pointed out that he was always met by chauffeur-driven limos wherever he went, and that to change his pattern now would create more problems than taking the chance that Mac and Ariel might be recognized by the driver.

Fortunately, despite a blue sky and brilliant sunshine, the early-morning mountain air was bitterly cold and provided ample justification for Mac to bury the lower half of his face in the cashmere scarf Ralph had given him, and for Ariel to hunch into the turned-up collar of Miranda's ski jacket.

The route from the Eagle-Vail airport to Beaver Creek took them right past the exit for Edwards, but Ariel realized they couldn't just zip off the highway and knock on doors asking if anyone knew Consuela. The FBI had done its job so well, she and Mac were almost as likely to be recognized in Colorado as in California. They would have to move very carefully if they were to avoid being clapped in jail before they discovered where Consuela was hiding out.

Although it was barely November, snow already blanketed the mountains, and Beaver Creek village glistened under a spun-sugar frosting of pristine snow. The architecture of the resort might be half kitsch, half fairy tale, but the background of soaring peaks, bare-branched aspen and brooding blue spruce made the views wholly spectacular. Ariel, however, would have enjoyed the natural beauty of the

Rockies a great deal more if she hadn't been aware of Mac's fast-growing tension.

"Another mile and we're there," Ralph said, hanging up his cellular phone as they drove toward the village center. "Fortunately, it's preseason. The ski lifts aren't open, and the inn has almost no guests, so I've told them to give us two suites on the top floor. Breakfast will be waiting for us when we arrive. I ordered your favorite Jamaican coffee, Ariel."

"Coffee sounds wonderful. Thanks, Ralph."

"You're welcome," he said gruffly. "I'm trying to find ways to apologize for being such a total ass last night. Anything else I can do for either of you?"

"Go about your business as if we're simply two administrative aides, here to help you sort out problems with the management team at the inn," Mac said. "We just need to keep the police off our backs until we can trace Consuela. It shouldn't be long before I find her."

Ariel was surprised that Mac expected their search to be successful so soon. "Has Pip managed to tap into the county records?" she asked.

Mac shook his head. "I've found nothing," he said tersely. "Pip hasn't been able to access a single file within the state of Colorado. We're shut out completely, every data system I try to access is guarded by an impenetrable barrier. I can't even determine something as simple as whether or not the supposed Frances Foster has paid taxes or bought property in Eagle County."

Ariel drew in a sharp breath. "Do you think Consuela's locked up the files?"

"It seems extremely likely, since I can't imagine anyone from your century who would have the ability to keep me out."

Ariel wasn't sure whether to feel relieved or worried at this evidence of Consuela's activity. "Isn't that good news?" she asked. "Doesn't it at least mean that she's here, and we're on the right track?"

"It's good news. It means we're on the right track," Mac agreed, and then fell silent.

She'd seen Mac laughing, puzzled, intrigued, tense and a host of other things, but this was the first time she'd ever seen him when he looked utterly implacable. The intensity of his concentration was almost tangible and definitely nerve-racking. Ariel laid her hand lightly on his forearm, and he turned to look at her, but his gaze remained focused inward, not really seeing her.

"There's something you're not telling me," she said. "Mac, what is it?"

"Nothing. Everything is going just as I anticipated."

For some reason, Ariel found that comment far from re-assuring. "In that case, tell me how you expect to find Consuela. If she's managed to lock you out of all the data banks in the entire state of Colorado, how are you going to trace where she's hiding?"

For a split second, his gaze focused on her. "It will all work out," he said vaguely.

"How? From what you've told me, Consuela's Pip is more powerful than yours. Doesn't that mean she'll always know what you're planning?"

"In the end, no computer is smarter than the person who is using it," Mac said. "How much longer till we're at the inn, Ralph?"

"Right around the next bend in the road. Two minutes, no more."

Mac was never vague, Ariel thought. Why was he suddenly afflicted with the inability to give straight answers to simple questions? And then she realized.

"Oh my God," she breathed. "You're not going to go looking for Consuela, are you? You never planned to hunt her down. You're just going to wait for her to come and find you."

He shrugged. "As you pointed out, caressa, her Pip is more powerful than mine. She can block her retinal pattern from me, but I have no way to block mine from her. Ever since Consuela escaped from me at the hospital, I have had no choice except to allow Consuela to find me. The trick has been to escape capture by your police long enough to force her to meet me in a time and place of my choosing."

Ariel licked lips that had suddenly become painfully dry. "She already knows we're here, doesn't she?"

Mac inclined his head. "Yes, she already knows. Pip warned me that I had been scanned ten minutes ago."

A muscle ticked in Ralph's normally expressionless face. Ariel wondered if she looked as nervous as her brother-in-law. "Could Pip tell where Consuela was scanning from?" Ralph asked. "Is she here in Colorado already?"

"Pip couldn't get a lock on the precise location of the scan, it was too fast, but I'm sure she's already here. Even the most powerful Pip can only make positive retinal identifications within a radius of about a hundred kilometers."

"If it's so easy for her to find you here in Colorado, why couldn't she find you in Los Angeles?" Ariel asked.

"The population of Greater Los Angeles is fourteen and a half million. The population of Edwards is less than a thousand. Imagine the computing power it takes to identify one person in fourteen and a half million, especially when your target is constantly moving. Now imagine how little power it takes to scan new arrivals at Eagle-Vail airport. You have computers in your own time that could easily do the job. For a Pip as powerful as Consuela's, it's child's play."

Ralph was looking inscrutable again, which Ariel realized was simply the expression he glued onto his face when he was worried half to death. "In the circumstances, Mac, wouldn't it have been smarter to stay in California?" he asked.

"Not at all," Mac said coolly. "Consuela and I both knew that it was only a matter of time before your FBI arrested me. So we both also knew I would have to find some way to induce her to confront me. As soon as she discovered that she'd dropped that fake driver's license, she knew I would make my way to Colorado and set myself up as her target. It was the only logical step for me to take."

Fear made Ariel angry. "Have you considered the fact that setting yourself up as the target for an assassin is a very easy way to get yourself killed?"

Mac smiled with none of his familiar warmth. "I don't plan to die, Ariel."

"And I'm sure Consuela will take your plans into consideration! But I don't suppose she plans to die, either!" Her throat had closed so tight, she could barely breathe, much less speak.

Mac touched her cheek. "It will all work out, caressa. I will take Consuela back to my world, and she will face trial, I promise you."

And that was supposed to make her feel better? Ariel hunched miserably against the soft leather of the car seat. It was depressing to realize that the very best outcome to their current situation was that Mac would avoid being killed—but disappear from her life forever. The worst possible outcome didn't even bear considering.

The Lincoln Town Car drew to a smooth halt outside Ralph's "little ski lodge," which turned out to be a giant resort hotel with an attractive pseudo-Alpine exterior and its own private lift up Beaver Creek Mountain. The driver hurried around to open the door for them. "Welcome to the High Country Inn," he said. "I hope you enjoy your stay here with us."

"Thanks," Ariel said, trying to keep the sarcasm out of her voice. "I'm sure we're going to love every minute of it."

THE GENERAL MANAGER escorted them to their adjoining suites, with two bellmen to carry their three small overnight bags, and a waiter from room service scurrying behind with a thermos jug of freshly brewed coffee. Ralph, accustomed to such service, gave no sign that he noticed their trail of escorts, but at least his presence meant that they were ushered through the lobby so fast, there was almost no time for staff or guests to recognize either Mac or Ariel.

Galvanized by the sheaf of faxes and phone messages waiting for him, Ralph grabbed a glass of juice from the laden buffet, and retired to a corner of one of the living rooms, where he soon seemed to be genuinely caught up in phoning colleagues all over the world, barking instructions and punching notes into his laptop computer. Making sure that your millions of dollars continued to generate more millions of dollars was obviously a nerve-racking and time-consuming business, Ariel thought, observing him with rueful affection.

With Ralph deep in a three-way conversation to Singapore and Hong Kong, Mac opened the door that led into the other suite so that he and Ariel could be alone. Guiding her to the window with its magnificent view of the snow-covered mountains, he put his arms around her and drew her close, his arms wrapped around her waist. "I wish we had time to walk up that mountain," he said, rubbing his cheek against her hair. "What a great morning activity that would be."

Ariel looked at the almost vertical slope of the mountain in front of the window, and laughed softly. "I never thought I'd say this, but thank God we have to wait for Consuela. I don't think either my lungs or my calf muscles are up to the climb."

There was an infinitesimal pause before Mac spoke. "We don't have to wait for Consuela," he said. "I do."

"What do you mean?"

"It is time for us to say goodbye, caressa." He spun her around in his arms so that they were facing each other, thigh to thigh, heart to heart. "I wish we could have met in a different time and place, but we didn't, and now I must leave you, at least for a while."

Ariel's heart lurched in denial. "You don't need to leave yet, Mac. Consuela isn't here."

He curved his hand against her cheek, his eyes dark with emotion. "But she is coming, caressa. Very soon."

"You don't know that for certain. We have a little while longer. Besides, I'm coming with you when you confront her, Mac. I can help you—"

He pressed his finger against her mouth, silencing the frantic flow of words. "Ariel, don't, please. We both know that I cannot risk your life by taking you with me. I must meet Consuela alone, in a place where she can do no harm to you or any other innocent bystander."

Ariel tore herself from Mac's arms and stared dry-eyed out of the window, her throat aching as she watched the sun sprinkle crystals of jeweled brightness on the snowy mountain. How ironic that she should come to such a beautiful place in order to feel such unbearable sadness. She wasn't ready to say goodbye to Mac. Somehow, she'd thought they would have a little longer together, a few more hours . . .

She would have insisted on accompanying him to confront Consuela if she hadn't known in her heart of hearts that her presence would only distract him from what he needed to do. The stark truth was that if she hadn't been with him at the hospital, Consuela would by now be in his custody, and Mac would already be back in the twenty-second century. She swallowed hard, choking down the bitter knowledge that

Mac would arrest Consuela, or die in the attempt, and she could do nothing to affect the outcome of that struggle.

He touched her on the shoulder. "I must go, Ariel."

She turned to look at him, and the words she'd thought were safely buried deep inside her broke through. "I love you, Mac. I wish you could stay in this time with me forever."

"I wish that, too," he said quietly. "You and your world are both very beautiful." He bent his head and kissed her with tender, aching passion. She kissed him back with a yearning so profound she felt engulfed by it.

"I love you, Ariel," he said and she heard the same edge of harsh regret in his voice that had been in her own. "I thank you for the time we have shared, and for the gift of your laughter."

She rested her head against his chest, feeling the slow beat of his heart for the last time. "Mac, please take care. I want to know that you're alive somewhere in the universe."

"I have every intention of staying alive, caressa. And when Consuela has faced her trial, I will come back to you, if you will have me."

She had never dared to hope for so much. She still didn't want to tempt fate by letting herself truly believe that he would return. "I'll be waiting," she said.

"By the ocean, where we first met, at midnight, on the eve of the new year. A great time for new beginnings." He kissed her again, whispering his final words against her mouth. "Think of me until I come back to you, caressa, and remember, I shall always love you."

He was walking away from her, and Ariel knew there were a hundred reasons why he would never return. A thousand reasons. She couldn't bear to watch him go. She closed her eyes and waited until she heard the door of the suite close. Then she leaned against the window until even the memory of his touch faded, and she felt nothing but the ice-cold glass at her back, and the hot, dry, centrally heated air sucking at the moisture in her lungs, making her gasp for breath. She turned, leaning her forehead against the glass, trying to imagine how she would endure a lifetime spent without Mac. A lifetime without ever knowing whether or not he'd successfully arrested Consuela. A lifetime without knowing if he was alive.

The sound of somebody opening the door to the suite had her spinning around, her heart pounding with anticipation. Oh, God, he'd come back! Did she want to go through another goodbye? Could she stand it?

"Mac . . ." Her voice died away to an astonished whisper. "Consuela!"

Her brain clicked into action a split second later. She was already yelling Ralph's name as she ran for the connecting door into his suite. Consuela, of course, ran faster. She intercepted Ariel in the middle of the room, knocking her out with a swift, backhanded uppercut to her jaw. The last thing Ariel saw was the ceiling dipping toward her, and Consuela's gleaming, triumphant smile.

IT WAS FREEZING COLD. Her body shook and her face burned with the cold. Her lungs ached from pumping the icy air in and out again. She wanted to sleep, to slide back into the darkness and the comforting illusion of warmth, but a buzzing in her head forced her eyes open. She made herself sit up and take stock because she knew that if she didn't find some way to warm herself, she would die.

With painful slowness, she viewed a world of blinding brightness and endless white. She was somewhere on the side of a mountain, Ariel realized, lying in a crevice, half covered by a bank of snow. But at least it was still full daylight, and she could see the chairs of the ski lift only a few feet away. If she followed the lift, there was a fighting chance that she'd be able to make her way down the slope before she froze to death. Wincing at a shooting pain in her much-abused ankle, she pulled herself to her feet, shoving her hands under her sweater in a desperate effort to ward off the chill.

"Going somewhere?" Consuela stepped out from behind a nearby rock. Dressed in a ski outfit that looked vaguely familiar, Ariel could only stare longingly at her adversary's thick down jacket and knitted cap. As far as she was concerned, even the gun Consuela was holding seemed of secondary importance to those beautiful warm clothes.

Teeth chattering, the shivering of her body verging on convulsions, Ariel attempted to speak. "W-why h-have you b-brought me h-here?"

"We're waiting for Robbie, and you're the bait for my trap." Consuela smiled condescendingly, as if her explanation would be obvious to anyone but a moron. "Don't try to run away, will you, because I'd have to shoot you in the leg, and I believe that would be quite painful. People from my century are squeamish, you know. We hate to inflict pain."

"Y-you'll k-kill me, anyway. What difference does it m-make whether it's now or later?"

"Don't be pessimistic, Ariel. While there's life, there's hope. Isn't that one of your quaint twentieth-century sayings?" Consuela took off her hat and shook out her gorgeous mane of hair. "Here, catch. Pip tells me we can expect Robbie to arrive in approximately eighty-two seconds and I don't want you passing out on me again. Pip had a hard enough job of waking you this time. I keep forgetting how inferior people's strength is in this century."

Ariel's hands were too numb to grasp anything, and the hat Consuela tossed toward her dropped onto the powdery snow. She would have liked to grind it into the ground and stomp on it for good measure, but common sense triumphed over pride and she picked up the hat, pulling the fur-lined flaps over her ears, grateful for the lingering heat of Consuela's body that momentarily warded off the bitter chill.

"You d-didn't need me to b-bait your t-trap. M-Mac was already searching for you."

"I'm sure he was. But before I come face-to-face with Robbie again, I want to be sure that the odds are in my favor. I'm a busy woman, and I need him out of my life. Permanently. Oops, here he comes, and right on schedule. Such a reliable man, my Robbie. Did you know that nobody has ever called him Robbie except me? All Silver Partners give each other a nickname that nobody else uses. Isn't that a sweet custom? It makes for great bonding, so they say." She grabbed Ariel, holding her with an iron grip around the waist, the gun resting against Ariel's temple. Instead of feeling terror, Ariel felt a bizarre moment of relief that Consuela was blocking the wind.

She heard the soft sigh of snow shifting, and assumed it was the sound of Mac's footsteps, but from her restricted angle of vision she couldn't catch a glimpse of him. Finally, she heard his voice coming from a spot above them. Even though she couldn't see him, and he was speaking in Spanglish so she couldn't understand the words, she had no difficulty recognizing the ice-cold fury of his tone.

Ariel felt the answering surge of white-hot rage that swept through Consuela. For a second, she was sure Consuela was going to take aim at Mac. But Consuela must have realized he was deliberately provoking her in order to give Ariel a chance to escape, and she caught hold of her rising temper.

"English, Robbie," Consuela said, her voice mocking. "We must use English so that your dear friend Ariel can understand what we're saying. Besides, I've never liked Spanglish. It's a constant reminder of the Great Famine, a language invented by the illiterate for the illiterate."

"Most languages are. That's what gives them their vitality." All the anger had been smoothed out of Mac's voice, leaving it flat and hard.

"Linguistics, Robbie? Are we going to stand on the side of a mountain and discuss the theory of linguistics?" Consuela laughed. "That's my boy, Robbie. Ever the would-be philosopher."

She turned slightly, so that Ariel was finally able to see Mac. He stood poised on a rocky ledge about ten feet above them, his close-fitting ski outfit reminiscent of the silver body paint he'd worn when she first saw him. His eyes were shielded by wraparound sunglasses, which emphasized the total lack of expression in his face. And the gun he carried was aimed straight at Consuela's head.

Ariel remembered the course in antique weapons Mac had taken in graduate school, and for a moment hope flared. It died stillborn. However great a shot Mac might be, with Consuela's gun held flush against her temple, any shot that killed Consuela would kill her, too.

"We seem to be at a standoff," Consuela said. "You can kill me, Robbie, but then you know that Ariel will die, too. I don't think you want dear little Ariel to die. In fact, I'm counting on it."

"Why count on something so uncertain? You would have had a better chance of killing me if you hadn't taken Ariel hostage," Mac said.

"True. But some things are even more important than seeing you dead, Robbie. Not very many, of course. But a few."

His aim at her head never wavered. "What, precisely, are you trying to achieve, Consuela?"

"A new life," she said. "And this time, I shall be the sister with all the power, not the other way around. With Manuela blazing all those trails ahead of me, my talents have always been underappreciated. Don't you think I'll make a good president of the United States, Robbie?"

What in the world was she talking about? Ariel wondered. President of the United States? Surely she wasn't deluded enough to think she could get herself elected president?

Mac was quicker to grasp what Consuela meant. "You're going to kill Erika Johansen," he said, his voice even flatter and harder than before. "You're going to kill her and then you're going to take her place."

Erika Johansen, Ariel thought. Of course! That was who Consuela had reminded her of earlier. There was a slight resemblance between the two women, which Consuela had emphasized by wearing a ski outfit similar in color and style to the one in Erika's Olympic photograph. No doubt Consuela planned to have plastic surgery to make her likeness to Erika perfect. And with a twenty-second-century Pip at her disposal, she could probably change every record that existed, official and unofficial, so that any discrepancies between Consuela's attributes and Erika's could be eliminated, altered or suppressed, from fingerprints right down to blood group.

Consuela didn't seem upset that Mac had realized what she planned to do. "I'm not going to kill Erika right away," she said, her voice as casual as if she were discussing the time she would eat lunch. "In fact, I'm not going to kill her until after she's elected to the Senate. Think of it, Robbie. Erika's going to know she's won a great election victory, against all the odds, and contrary to the predictions of all the pollsters. She's going to die a very happy woman, don't you think?"

Only the absolute stillness of his body betrayed the intensity of Mac's reaction. "Even you, Consuela, can't believe that I'm going to let you get away with murdering two presidents."

She chuckled. "You don't have a choice, Robbie. There's nothing you can do to stop me."

"I can kill you," he said. "And I will."

"What about your dear friend Ariel?"

"I shall mourn her death," he said with clipped, emotionless precision.

Ariel looked at him, stunned.

"And that's it? Damn you, Robbie, is nothing more important to you than your damned professional honor?"

Mac shifted his weight, adjusting the aim of his gun to correct for Consuela's movements. "If you have some sort of deal to propose, Consuela, you'd better offer it very soon. I plan to pull the trigger on this gun within the next sixty seconds. It's a .44 Magnum. Inefficient by our standards, but deadly, as you probably know."

Ariel wished that his voice hadn't held quite such a convincing ring of truth, because if Consuela died, there didn't seem much chance of her surviving.

Consuela seemed to realize that Mac was serious and that time was running out for her. "Okay," she said. "Here's the deal, Mac. You will set the coordinates on your Pip to transport you back to 2196 where you belong. I will set the coordinates on my Pip to take Ariel with you, at the precise same moment. That way, I get to become president of the United States, and you two lovebirds get the chance to live together in mutual bliss for the rest of your lives. It's a great deal, Mac. Grab it, fast."

"You're offering the impossible," Mac said, but there was an edge of strain in his voice that hadn't been there before. "We both know that the time-travel chamber will only accept back life-forms it has sent out. Ariel would never survive the journey."

"Since I was the director in chief of time-travel research, you should know that I'm not going to suggest a time transfer that's impossible."

"How would you plan to overcome the refusal of the time-travel chamber to accept Ariel?" Mac asked brusquely.

"My Pip has already scanned and recorded Ariel's precise cellular structure. At my command, her biomolecular pattern can be injected into the nodule within my Pip that contains the record of my journey back in time. I can instruct Pip to substitute Ariel's molecular pattern for mine, while keeping all the other information unchanged. Then I will activate the return command, and—presto—the time-travel chamber will be deceived, and Ariel Hutton will end up in 2196 along with you."

Transporting to 2196 and living happily ever after with Mac definitely beat dying in 1996 with a bullet through her skull, but Ariel wasn't getting her hopes up. She had no idea if Consuela's suggestion made any sort of scientific sense, but she had a pretty clear idea that Consuela was far more likely trying to trick Mac than genuinely offering a deal.

Mac obviously thought the same. "I'm not a physicist, but I'm not a fool, either. What you're suggesting has never been tried. It sounds reasonable, but how do we know it would work?"

"We don't," Consuela said. "But consider the alternatives."

"I am considering them. If I kill you now, at least I know that Erika Johansen will be able to fulfill the role for which she is destined."

Consuela gave an impatient sigh. "Robbie, stop being such a damn hero for a few seconds. What do you care about events that ended more than a hundred years before you were born? What does it matter to you if the Erika Johansen who becomes the first woman president of the United States isn't actually the woman who was born Erika Johansen?"

"It matters a lot," Mac said. "For one thing, your impersonation of the real Erika Johansen would be changing the course of history. I might go back to 2196 and find that the society we both grew up in no longer exists because your murder of Erika Johansen has changed the past."

"You're assuming that my becoming president changes the past," Consuela said. "How do you know that the deeds of Erika Johansen recorded in the history books are not actually my deeds? How do you know that this wonderful, revered president is not actually me? Perhaps by allowing me to take the place of the real Erika Johansen, you are in fact fulfilling historical destiny, not perverting it."

There was a horrible, twisted logic to what Consuela was suggesting, Ariel realized. What's more, there was absolutely no way to prove that the woman who was born Erika Johansen in Edwards, Colorado, was the woman who had become the famous twenty-first century president. What if by insisting on transporting Consuela back to face trial in 2196, Mac was actually changing history, not preserving it?

Mac didn't answer for quite a while. "Perhaps you're right," he said, his voice apparently reflecting some of the uncertainty Ariel was feeling. "Maybe President Johansen was able to make such brilliant decisions because she knew that the Great Famine was coming. In some ways, considering the wisdom of her choices, it does seem almost as if she must have known the future. Maybe she really was you."

"At last you're seeing things from my point of view." Consuela was triumphant. "And so, Robbie, you'd better rethink your plan to haul me back to face trial, or your precious United Republic of the Americas isn't going to fare so well during the Great Famine. What will happen when the crops fail, and two hundred million new mouths are waiting to be fed, if President Johansen's food synthesizers haven't been brought into operation?"

"It's hard for me to accept that it may be my duty to allow you to go free, to give you the chance to murder Erika Johansen." Mac's voice wasn't quite steady. "I don't know what to do."

"Go home," Consuela said at once. "Set your Pip to take you home, and I'll send Ariel with you, just as I promised."

"Even if I agree that it's best to leave you here, how do I know you'll keep your word about Ariel?" Mac asked. "I may not be an expert on the physics of time travel, but I'm also not a fool. Before I activate the return program on my Pip, I want to verify that you've substituted Ariel's cellular patterns for your own. I'm not going to program myself out of here and then arrive back in 2196 only to discover that you haven't sent Ariel with me."

Ariel had known Mac for a matter of days. Consuela had known him for months, and the other woman seemed to detect nothing amiss with Mac's sudden burst of cooperation. Ariel, however, was willing to stake her life—literally—on the fact that the man she had fallen in love with would never agree to escape to safety, taking Ariel with him, and leaving Erika Johansen as a walking target for Consuela's murderous schemes. She marveled that Consuela didn't seem to see even a little way beneath the surface of his replies.

"All right, I'll allow your Pip to scan the data in my Pip," Consuela said finally.

Mac shook his head. "Get real, Consuela. Your Pip is so much more powerful than mine, it could falsify all the data and I would never know."

"Then what's your suggestion?"

"That you allow my Pip to download the necessary data so that I'm the one who controls the transfer of Ariel as well as myself."

"Don't be ridiculous—"

"There's no danger to you," Mac said. "You can isolate the time-travel data so that my Pip has no access to anything else. You know the precise limitations of my Pip. You know that there's absolutely no way that I could possibly overcome the safety barriers your Pip is capable of erecting."

"That's true," Consuela muttered, almost to herself.

Mac lowered his gun a fraction. "Pip is reporting to me that Ralph Dunnett is at the foot of the ski lift. He has three people with him, probably police officers. No doubt your Pip is reporting the same. You'd better hurry up and decide whether or not you're going to let me download that transportation program, Consuela, or we're all going to be dead."

There was a great clanking sound as the ski lift jolted and shuddered into operation. Consuela hesitated for no more than a moment. "Okay," she said. "We'll do it your way, Robbie."

She muttered a brief command to her Pip, then spoke to Mac. "Go ahead, I've released the security barrier on that one program. Your Pip can now download the necessary data to transport Ariel forward to 2196."

"Thank you, Consuela." To Ariel, the total absence of expression in Mac's voice was as revealing as blatant excitement would have been. She didn't understand a word of Mac's instructions to his Pip, but she knew that somehow, in some way, Consuela had just surrendered the weapons for her own defeat.

Mac's Pip beeped one final time and then fell silent. "Everything seems to be correct," Mac said.

"Of course it's correct." Consuela jerked impatiently at Ariel's neck. "For heaven's sake, Robbie, there are four people now riding up the mountain in the ski lift. Would you activate your program, and get the hell out of here before they arrive?"

"With pleasure," Mac said. "On the count of three. Remember, Ariel, New Year's Eve."

There was a flash of light, and a shimmer in the atmosphere as if space momentarily blurred. When the world righted itself again, Mac and Consuela had both disappeared and Ariel was alone on the side of the mountain, with the ski lift clanging overhead.

12

New Year's Eve, 1996

MIRANDA WISHED there was something she could do to lift the sadness that always seemed to haunt her sister's eyes these days. "Was the shopping trip successful?" she asked. "Did you find a new dress for the party tonight?"

"Yes, and it was on sale. Post-Christmas markdown, I guess. It'll be very useful for a variety of functions." Ariel opened the box and shook out the folds of black silk and lace, holding it up against her. "What do you think?"

Miranda pulled a face. "I think it looks horribly like every evening dress you've ever bought since high school," she said.

The sadness in Ariel's eyes seemed even more pronounced when she tried to smile. "Hey, that must prove I really like it!"

"Have you ever considered that there is an entire rainbow of colors other than black? And with your gorgeous coloring, several dozen of them must suit you."

Ariel leaned down and dropped a kiss on her sister's cheek. "Face it, Miranda, I'm a fashion disaster. But you can tell me how to fix my hair and makeup tonight. That should provide you with more than enough excitement for a woman who's five months pregnant with twins."

Ariel was so determined to be brave and sensible, Miranda wasn't sure whether to cry in sympathy or give her a good hard kick in the pants in the hope of knocking some sense into her. Ariel's resolute refusal to talk about Mac was definitely not helping her to forget him, Miranda was quite sure of that. Ariel had taken thirty-three years to fall in love, and when she'd finally done it, she'd fallen hard.

Maybe it was time to stop being tactful, Miranda reflected. It was crazy that neither she nor Ralph could find the courage to broach the topic that had been foremost in their minds for days. "It's New Year's Eve tonight," she said, drawing a deep breath and crossing her fingers for good measure.

Ariel smiled so brightly her face looked as if it might crack. "I know. You're giving one of your fabulous parties, and I've just bought a new dress to wear, remember?"

This time, Miranda refused to be shut out. "Do you think he'll come back?" she asked.

At least Ariel didn't pretend not to know what her sister was talking about. "I don't know," she said, crumpling the tissue her dress had been packed in. Reluctantly, she added. "I'm here, where he asked me to be."

Her voice rejected sympathy and probing, but now that they'd finally broached the forbidden topic, Miranda realized that her sister was hanging on to her self-control by the most slender of threads. "He'll come back to you if he can, Ariel, I'm sure of that much."

Ariel swung away, wrapping her arms around her waist as if she wanted to hold back the words that threatened to burst out of her. In the end, the dam broke, and the words poured out of her as if she couldn't bear to hold them in a moment longer. "What happens if he doesn't come? What does that mean?" she said. "It's the lack of closure that bothers me most. It would be bad enough if I just had to live with the fact that I fell in love with a man I'll probably never see again. I guess that happens to women all the time. But it's the not knowing that gets to me. Can you imagine what it's like to lie awake at night wondering whether Mac's disappearance was a triumph or a disaster? Is he alive? Is Consuela alive? And did we save the world or set it on the course to disaster?"

"I wish I could answer you," Miranda said. "And we may never know the answers to those questions. But maybe the important thing to remember is that you and Mac did everything within your power to make things turn out right. Isn't that all you can ever ask of yourself, or anyone?"

"I don't know," Ariel said. "Maybe I'm greedy, but I want more. I know we did our best, all of us, you and Ralph included. That's terrific, and I'm grateful, but I need to know if our best was good enough."

Miranda put her arms around her sister, and was relieved when Ariel returned the hug. "Try not to be too devastated if Mac doesn't come tonight, will you, sweetie? Sometimes, over the past couple of months, I've had the feeling that your whole life is on hold, waiting for Mac."

Ariel gave a smile of such determined cheerfulness that it nearly broke Miranda's heart. "Of course I won't be devastated if Mac doesn't come tonight," she said. "I just want New Year's Eve to be over, so that I can get on with the rest of my life."

IF ONLY she could make herself believe her own lies, Ariel thought as she reclaimed her velvet wrap from an attendant and walked away from the lights and noise of the party into the chill darkness of the gardens. Ralph saw her leave and followed her out of the house onto the patio where a few guests had braved the cold to smoke cigarettes. "Do you want me to come with you?" he asked. "You might need some moral support."

"No," she said. "But thanks for asking, Ralph."

"You're welcome. And don't forget, Ariel. Miranda and I are always here if you need us."

She thanked him again and walked slowly down the path toward the sea, wondering how she could ever have found Miranda's relationship with her husband mysterious. Ralph loved Miranda almost to distraction, and Miranda returned his love with equal intensity. His calm anchored her exuberance, and her liveliness lifted his spirits. It was strange to think that only two months ago her sensitivity to other people's emotions had been so blunted that she'd been unable to figure out that her own sister was passionately in love. Falling in love had sure done a great job of enabling her to see the world from an entirely new perspective. She'd even managed to accept the kelp cookies her mother had sent her for Christmas without so much as a murmur of exasperation.

She looked at her watch. Eleven o'clock. By this time on Halloween night, Mac had already been here. Ariel leaned against the wall and stared down at the white-crested waves of the Pacific hurling themselves against the rocks. For once, the endless vista of sea and sky had no power to calm her. A sudden gust of wind had her pulling her velvet wrap more tightly around her, glad of its warmth.

As quickly as the breeze had sprung up, it died away again, leaving her corner of the garden undisturbed. Except that she wasn't alone anymore, Ariel realized. A man, with dark hair and brilliant blue eyes, seemed to materialize right out of the center of the clump of oleander bushes that grew to her left, against the wall. He pushed the branches apart, pulling dark green leaves out of his hair. Then he saw Ariel, and his face broke into a huge smile.

"Mac!" She breathed his name on a sigh of such overflowing happiness that her whole being threatened to shatter. "Mac! You're here!"

She ran toward him, and he swept her off her feet, swinging her high above his head before pulling her into his arms and smothering her with kisses.

"You waited for me," he said when they finally stopped kissing each other long enough to speak.

"You came back," she said, resting her head against his chest and breathing in the familiar, heady scent of him.

"I even wore clothes," he said, gesturing to his outfit.

"Pants and a shirt. And shoes, too. I'm impressed. You look very handsome."

"And you look very beautiful. I like your dress. It reminds me of the one you were wearing when first we met."

She laughed, but when he asked her to explain what was amusing, she shook her head and took his hand, walking with him to the wall. "I'll explain later about the dress. But before we go inside, tell me what happened back there on the mountain, Mac. What happened to you and Consuela?"

"We arrived safely in my own world and I formally arrested her on a charge of high treason. She was tried and found guilty."

"Will she be executed?" Ariel asked.

"No, we don't have the death penalty, but she'll be imprisoned for life in a maximum-security jail and believe me, our technology leaves no chance of escape."

"How did you do it?" Ariel asked. "How in the world did you manage to take her back?"

He shrugged. "It wasn't too difficult once she gave me access to her Pip. She had spoken the truth when she claimed to have programmed her time-travel nodule to transport you back to 2196 with me. What she must have forgotten is that the Pip I was carrying had been a gift from her sister, intended for Consuela's and my mutual pleasure, so naturally it had been preprogrammed with Consuela's molecular- and cellular-identification patterns. Once I'd downloaded the coordinates and parameters of her jounrey, it was the work of an instant for me to reconfigure the time-travel program so that it once again carried her cellular patterns, not yours. Therefore, when I activated the transport command, it was Consuela who accompanied me back to 2196, not you."

"Somehow, I don't think what you did was quite as simple as you make it sound," she said.

He stroked her hair tenderly. "I discovered that terror can be a great stimulus to creative thinking. When I realized that Consuela wasn't chasing me, but had doubled back in order to take you hostage, I was frantic. I hope I never have to live through another half hour as terrible as the one climbing up that mountain in pursuit of you and Consuela."

"Did we do the right thing?" she asked him. "I know that Consuela had committed a terrible crime in your century, and that you wanted her to stand trial, but what if she was right, Mac, and history intended for her to kill Erika Johansen and take her place as president? There could be millions of future lives riding on our decisions, Mac."

He brushed his hand across her forehead, smoothing out her frown. "I am sure that you need have no worries on that score, caressa. Whatever I may have pretended for Consuela's benefit, I never for one instant doubted that history intends Erika Johansen to become president of the United States."

"How can you be so sure?"

"President Johansen had many admirers, and a few who disagreed with her views completely, just like any other politician. But everyone who met her agreed her integrity was absolute and that she was honest to a fault. You and I both know that Consuela could never have convinced an entire nation of her honesty, or her rock-solid integrity. Whatever role she was playing, whatever personality she assumed, her basic moral weakness would always have shown through. I think you can be sure that when Consuela was transported back to 2196, we not only returned a murderer to justice, we also prevented a disastrous perversion of history."

A burden Ariel had begun to find almost too heavy to carry felt as if it had been lifted from her back. They'd done the right thing, and the good guys had won. Erika Johansen—the real Erika Johansen—would be a great president and help save America from the worst effects of the Great Famine. Ariel could stop worrying about the nation's future and start enjoying her own.

Lighthearted, dizzy with excitement, she stood on tiptoe and kissed Mac with all the pent-up passion of their long weeks of separation. He lifted her high, holding her tightly as he kissed her back with a desire and longing that matched her own.

Overhead, the sky lit up in a burst of golden light, and the crack of exploding rockets heralded the end of the old year, and the start of the new. "It must be midnight," she said to him, her happiness as shimmering and exciting as the fireworks lighting up the sky. "Happy New Year, Mac."

He looked down at her naked face, made rosy by the shower of red sparkles cascading from the clouds, and knew he had found the place in time where he was meant to be. "Happy New Year, caressa."

She laughed. "I love fireworks, don't you? Do you celebrate the new year with fireworks in your world, Mac?"

"This is my world," he said softly. "Yours and mine, caressa. For the rest of our lives."

UNLOCK THE DOOR TO GREAT ROMANCE AT BRIDE'S BAY RESORT

Join Harlequin's new across-the-lines series, set in an exclusive hotel on an island off the coast of South Carolina.

Seven of your favorite authors will bring you exciting stories about fascinating heroes and heroines discovering love at Bride's Bay Resort.

Look for these fabulous stories coming to a store near you beginning in January 1996.

Harlequin American Romance #613 in January
Matchmaking Baby by Cathy Gillen Thacker

Harlequin Presents #1794 in February
Indiscretions by Robyn Donald

Harlequin Intrigue #362 in March
Love and Lies by Dawn Stewardson

Harlequin Romance #3404 in April
Make Believe Engagement by Day Leclaire

Harlequin Temptation #588 in May
Stranger in the Night by Roseanne Williams

Harlequin Superromance #695 in June
Married to a Stranger by Connie Bennett

Harlequin Historicals #324 in July
Dulcie's Gift by Ruth Langan

Visit Bride's Bay Resort each month wherever
Harlequin books are sold.

MILLION DOLLAR SWEEPSTAKES

SWP-H296

Are your lips succulent, impetuous, delicious or racy?

Find out in a very special Valentine's Day promotion—THAT SPECIAL KISS!

Inside four special Harlequin and Silhouette February books are details for THAT SPECIAL KISS! explaining how you can have your lip prints read by a romance expert.

Look for details in the following series books, written by four of Harlequin and Silhouette readers' favorite authors:

Silhouette Intimate Moments #691
Mackenzie's Pleasure by *New York Times* bestselling author Linda Howard

Harlequin Romance #3395
Because of the Baby by Debbie Macomber

Silhouette Desire #979
Megan's Marriage by Annette Broadrick

Harlequin Presents #1793
The One and Only by Carole Mortimer

Fun, romance, four top-selling authors, plus a **FREE** gift! This is a very special Valentine's Day you won't want to miss! Only from Harlequin and Silhouette.

VAL96

Women throughout time have
lost their hearts to:

Starting in January 1996, Harlequin Temptation
will introduce you to five irresistible, sexy rogues.
Rogues who have carved out their place in history,
but whose true destinies lie in the arms of
contemporary women.

#569 *The Cowboy*, Kristine Rolofson
(January 1996)

#577 *The Pirate*, Kate Hoffmann
(March 1996)

#585 *The Outlaw*, JoAnn Ross
(May 1996)

#593 *The Knight*, Sandy Steen
(July 1996)

#601 *The Highwayman*, Madeline Harper
(September 1996)

Dangerous to love, impossible to resist!

You're About to Become a *Privileged Woman*

Reap the rewards of fabulous free gifts and benefits with proofs-of-purchase from Harlequin and Silhouette books

Pages & Privileges™

It's our way of thanking you for buying our books at your favorite retail stores.

PROOF OF PURCHASE
Offer expires October 31, 1996
HT-PP103

Harlequin and Silhouette—
the most privileged readers in the world!

For more information about Harlequin and Silhouette's PAGES & PRIVILEGES program call the Pages & Privileges Benefits Desk: 1-503-794-2499

HARLEQUIN®